MW01273686

ISSUES THAT CONCERN YOU

Social Protest

Arthur Gillard, *Book Editor*

Okanagan Mission Secondary
4544 Gordon Drive
Kelowna, B.C. V1W 1T4

GREENHAVEN PRESS
A part of Gale, Cengage Learning

GALE
CENGAGE Learning·

Farmington Hills, Mich • San Francisco • New York • Waterville, Maine
Meriden, Conn • Mason, Ohio • Chicago

Elizabeth Des Chenes, *Director, Content Strategy*
Cynthia Sanner, *Publisher*
Douglas Dentino, *Manager, New Product*

Articles in Greenhaven Press anthologies are often edited for length to meet page requirements. In addition, original titles of these works are changed to clearly present the main thesis and to explicitly indicate the author's opinion. Every effort is made to ensure that Greenhaven Press accurately reflects the original intent of the authors. Every effort has been made to trace the owners of copyrighted material.

Cover image © Eric Crama/ShutterStock.com.

LIBRARY OF CONGRESS CATALOGING-IN-PUBLICATION DATA

Social protest / Arthur Gillard, book editor.
    pages cm. -- (Issues that concern you)
Includes bibliographical references and index.
ISBN 978-0-7377-6934-0 (hardcover)
1. Protest movements--United States--Juvenile literature. 2. Social movements--United States--Juvenile literature. 3. Political participation--United States--Juvenile literature.
I. Gillard, Arthur.
HN65.S5764 2014
303.48'4--dc23
    2014002608

CONTENTS

The United States has a rich history of social protest movements that have created positive change in society—the nineteenth-century abolitionist movement to free the slaves, the twentieth-century civil rights movements that ended racial segregation and garnered women's rights, and more. Arguably the first social protest movement in the United States was the resistance movement against British rule that led to the Revolutionary War and the founding of the country. Throughout the entire history of the United States, social protest movements large and small have left their mark on the culture and politics of the nation, striving to improve life for particular groups or society as a whole, according to the particular vision of each movement. Progressive movements have often been met with conservative movements that attempt to maintain the status quo, to preserve traditional values, or to prevent what is seen as a dangerous wrong turn for society. Significant recent movements include the medical marijuana movement, the Tea Party movement advocating for a reduction in government spending and taxation, the Occupy movement of 2011 that drew attention to wealth inequality in the United States, and the increasingly successful movement to secure full equality for gays and lesbians.

Currently, there are three broad trends fueling protest movements, each of which has the potential to become much bigger in years and decades to come: wealth inequality, widespread surveillance (privacy), and climate change.

Wealth inequality became a central issue in 2011 with the Occupy movement, which popularized the terms *the 1%* (the wealthiest Americans, with a net worth of around $7 million or more) and *the 99%* (everyone else), speaking to the widespread perception that the richest 1 percent of the population wields a disproportionate amount of the wealth and power in the United States. Many people noticed that after the economic crash of 2008, which caused millions of people to lose their homes and/or their jobs, bankers and heads of corporations were richly rewarded despite bearing much responsibility for the financial crisis. As Nobel Prize–winning economist Joseph E. Stiglitz notes,

> Around the world, the financial crisis unleashed a new sense of unfairness, or more accurately, a new realization that our economic system was unfair, a feeling that had been vaguely felt in the past but now could no longer be ignored. . . . What happened undermined the prevailing justification for inequality, that those who made greater contributions to society receive (and should receive) larger rewards. Bankers reaped large rewards even though their contribution to society—and even to their firms—had been *negative*. In other sectors, CEOs who ran their firms into the ground, causing losses for shareholders and workers alike, were rewarded with gargantuan bonuses.[1]

Although the stock market has recovered since then, conditions for large segments of the population continue to worsen, creating conditions ripe for further protest movements targeting inequality.

Environmental issues in general, and climate change in particular, have been the subject of popular protest movements for several decades, but despite this the threat to the environment continues unabated. According to scientists and organizations studying the issue, as time goes on without addressing the problem of climate change, the threat to civilization and perhaps human survival itself becomes increasingly dire. Meanwhile the unfolding of climate change in the real world has resulted, according to a study by Stanford University professor Jon Krosnick in 2013, in a vast majority of Americans now believing that climate change is real and wanting decisive action taken to address the problem. Despite this, governments around the world have done nothing substantial to address the problem; while scientists call for immediate and strong reductions in carbon dioxide emissions (the putative main driver of climate change), such emissions continue to increase. In recent years protests demanding more action against climate

From the early days of the republic to the present day, social protest has been an avenue for seeking reform.

change have been increasing in intensity, and there is every reason to believe that trend will continue, and likely increase, in the years and decades to come. It is an issue of particular importance to young people; as Alec Loorz, who became an environmental activist when he was twelve, points out, "Youth have a unique sense of moral authority on this issue [climate change]. It's our planet now. And we are going to have to grow up and face the consequences of what the world does, or fails to do."[2]

Since 2001, there has been an increasing amount of government surveillance of the population in the name of fighting terrorism, accompanied by secret laws, secret courts, torture, and indefinite detainment of people suspected of terrorist activities or connections. This has predictably led to resistance and protest movements against the erosion of civil liberties. Following revelations by whistleblower Edward Snowden in 2013 of widespread and pervasive surveillance by the National Security Agency (NSA) of the entire US population as well as of citizens and leaders of other countries around the world, public outrage and opposition to such programs—both in the United States and elsewhere—has increased dramatically. As of early 2014, neither the NSA nor the federal government appears to have any intention of curtailing such surveillance, creating the likelihood that protest movements to protect privacy and freedom will continue to increase in the years to come.

Widespread surveillance is a matter of particular concern for activists and protesters, who regularly oppose powerful forces in society. Knowing that secretive agencies and governments are watching the population as a whole (and dissidents, activists, and protesters in particular) creates a chilling effect on protest movements or even on the discussing of topics that are likely to be controversial or seen as suspicious by authorities. Organizations such as the American Civil Liberties Union (ACLU) and Electronic Frontier Foundation (EFF) are fighting to protect freedom and privacy by attempting to sharply limit the amount of surveillance that can be carried out by intelligence organizations, either through trying to get laws passed limiting such activities or by promoting the use of tools such as encryption that supposedly protect ordinary people from surveillance. Critics of this approach point out that as long as agencies such as the NSA are allowed to operate in secret there will be no meaningful way to limit spying on the public in general and activists in particular. Consequently there is a growing movement promoting "watching the watchers" using increasingly widespread recording technology (for example, smartphones) to record the activities of the police and other authorities. Whistleblowers such as Chelsea (formerly Bradley) Manning and Edward Snowden are also part of this increasingly widespread movement, as are hackers such as Jeremy Hammond, sentenced to ten years in prison for hacking into Stratfor (Strategic Forecasting, a global intelligence firm) and releasing 3 million e-mails (which allegedly revealed, among other things, attempts to falsely link particular protesters to terrorist groups in order to prosecute them as terrorists).

Climate change, surveillance, wealth inequality, civil rights, drug prohibition—there are many important causes in the world today to get involved in. Young political activist Christina Wong of Sacramento, California, notes, "If everyone helped out with one cause that they believed in—the environment, health care, civil rights—the world would be in much better shape than it is right now."[3]

Although at times it may seem hopeless to meaningfully address the many problems in the world, there is much that can be done to improve the situation. In the worlds of activist Aaron Swartz,

> What's going on now isn't some reality TV show you can just sit at home and watch. This is your life, this is your country—and if you want to keep it safe, you need to get involved. . . .
>
> I know it's easy to feel like you're powerless, like there's nothing you can do to slow down or stop "the system." Like all the calls are made by shadowy and powerful forces far outside your control. I feel that way, too, sometimes. But it just isn't true. . . .
>
> The system is changing. Thanks to the Internet, everyday people can learn about and organize around an issue even if the system is determined to ignore it. Now, maybe we won't win every time—this is real life, after all—but we finally have a chance.[4]

As Julia Butterfly Hill, an environmental activist who spent more than two years living in a fifteen-hundred-year-old California redwood tree in a successful bid to protect it from a logging company, points out, "Now more than ever in our collective story, we need as many of us as possible to stand up and be courageous in our vision. Each one of us is a unique gift and each role we play is equal in importance. What is challenging for me is a walk in the park for someone else and vice versa. It is up to you to step into your greatest self—who you are is who you are meant to be and your contribution is vital."[5]

Authors in this anthology offer a variety of perspectives on social protest. In addition, the volume contains several appendixes to help the reader understand and further explore the topic, including a thorough bibliography and a list of organizations to contact for further information. The appendix titled "What You Should Know About Social Protest" offers facts about the subject. The appendix "What You Should Do About Social Protest" offers advice for action for young people who are concerned with this issue. With all these features, *Issues That Concern You: Social Protest* provides an excellent resource for everyone interested in this increasingly important topic.

Notes

1. Quoted in Anya Schiffrin and Eamon Kircher-Allen, eds., *From Cairo to Wall Street: Voices from the Global Spring.* New York: New Press, 2012, pp. 4–7.
2. Quoted in Sharon J. Smith, *The Young Activist's Guide to Building a Green Movement + Changing the World.* Berkeley, CA: Ten Speed, 2011, p. 52.
3. Quoted in Smith, *The Young Activist's Guide*, p. 88.
4. Quoted in Cory Doctorow, *Homeland.* New York: Tor Teen, 2013, pp. 270–271.
5. Quoted in Smith, *The Young Activist's Guide*, p. viii.

ONE

An Overview of Protest Movements

Leonard Gordon

> Leonard Gordon is a former dean and professor at Arizona State University and the author of *A City in Racial Crisis: Detroit Pre and Post the 1967 Riot.* In the following viewpoint Gordon argues that protest movements occur when people want change that individually they are powerless to bring about and so work with other like-minded people to achieve the desired change. When protest happens on a large scale, significant changes in society can result, but according to Gordon, this often leads to *countermovements*, in which groups of people within government or society at large work to oppose the changes championed by the protest movement. For example, the women's rights movement succeeded in improving economic and political equality for women, but countermovements have slowed progress considerably. Gordon notes that protesters use a variety of strategies and that the results of protest movements are often unpredictable.

The twentieth century has been characterized by a wide variety of protest movements. In the United States, industrial protests were common for the first third of the century, as were anti-immigration protests. The suffragette protest movement early

Leonard Gordon, "Protest Movements," *Encyclopedia of Sociology, 2nd ed.*, vol. 3, Macmillan Reference USA, 2001, pp. 2265–2272. *Encyclopedia of Sociology*, 2E. Copyright © 2001 Gale, a part of Cengage Learning, Inc. Reproduced by permission. www.cengage.com/permissions.

in the century was a precursor to the women's movement for equal treatment and opportunity in the last third of the century. The civil rights movement, led by blacks in the 1950s and 1960s, precipitated countermovements—a common characteristic of protest movements—including the White Citizen's Council protests [opposing racial integration in schools] and the reemergence of the Ku Klux Klan [hooded white supremacist group]. Poor people in Chile, El Salvador, Nicaragua, and other Latin American countries have protested the privileges of an elite economic class. . . . Such protest movements are evident globally, with protest occurrences in Africa, the Middle East, and Asia.

A common thread through the wide variety of protest movements is their political nature. In various ways governmental authority is challenged, changed, supported, or resisted in specific protest movements. To advance their prospects for success, protest movement leaders often engage in coalition politics with more powerful individuals and groups who, for their own interests and values, support the challenge raised by the movement. When protest movements succeed in generating sufficient public support to secure all or most of their goals, governments may offer policy legitimization of the movement as a means of adapting to, coopting, or modifying a movement's challenge to the state of premovement affairs.

Such political legitimation has taken a variety of forms. The labor protest movements culminated in the passage of the National Labor Relations Act of 1935, which legitimized labor-management collective bargaining and negotiated agreements. The suffragette movement resulted in passage of the Nineteenth Amendment to the Constitution, guaranteeing that the right to vote in the United States could not be denied or abridged on account of [a citizen's] sex. The civil rights movement attained support with passage of the comprehensive Civil Rights Act in 1964 and then the Economic Opportunity Act and the Elementary and Secondary Education Act, both in 1965. All these system-modifying acts, which affect the lives of millions in American society, have continued in effect during relatively high and low periods of public support. This gives evidence of the long-term societal legitimation of these acts, which grew out of protest movements.

Countermovements

Success of these and other movements is often tempered by countermovements, participants in which perceive their relative positions and interests to be threatened. For instance, the women's movement experienced a series of challenges from religious groups, often fundamentalist, that adhered to a male-dominated patriarchy. As a consequence, women's progress was slowed in winning various forms of equal treatment and opportunity in educational, economic, political, and social areas of life, and in the 1970s and the 1980s Congress failed to pass the Equal Rights Amendment (ERA) to the U.S. Constitution, which was supported by the women's movement.

More generally, after passage of civil rights legislation in the mid-1960s, a series of protest movements within the Democratic and, more extensively, the Republican parties resulted in growing administrative, legislative, and judicial resistance to equality in educational, occupational, and housing opportunities. The countermovement result has been a reentrenchment of a long-established economic structure of racism and low-income class rigidity. . . .

When protests and counterprotests result in social change, such change generally affects the participants in a specific protest movement as well as established authorities in ways often not fully anticipated. . . .

Protest movements attain mixed and sometimes changed results. These results occur because of institutional inertia, in which certain things have been done certain ways over a long period of time, and because of countermovements within institutional centers such as schools; businesses; and local, state, and national government offices. In the United States, reactions to the civil rights movement have resulted in private and public attitudes and behavior that have combined to support inclusion of some minority members while disadvantaging more severely the lowest-income racial and ethnic minorities. The result is that the countermovement resistance to educational, economic, and political advances for minority status groups has adversely affected the poorest racial and ethnic minority members. At the

A 1913 poster announces a march in Washington, DC, for women's right to vote.

same time, census bureau reports document a growing number and proportion of blacks, women, and other minority group members moving into educational institutions, occupational settings, and political positions from which they were formerly excluded. . . .

Examples from history and other cultures demonstrate the mixed potential and results of protest movements. The German Nazi protest movement in the 1920s illustrated that a movement could be radical *and* reactionary, in that case toward further destabilization of the Weimar Republic's democratic government, which was perceived as being decreasingly effective and legitimate by growing sectors of the German public. . . . An historic, more recent example is the 1989 Chinese student democratic movement in Tianenmen Square that resulted in a government-sponsored countermovement that physically shattered the student protest and created a system of political, economic, and educational controls that were more comprehensively rigid than those that existed before the protest movement. Yet, the underlying educational, economic, and political forces that generated the Chinese student activists continued to affect the dynamics of Chinese society, with the potential for further protest activation.

In these and other protest movements, there is a wide range of participants and of protest methods employed. . . .

Protest Participants and Methods of Protest

If protest participants could alleviate their grievances or sense of injustice individually, there would be no likely motivation for them to become active in a protest movement. Protest participants thus have two central characteristics: (1) they have insufficient influence to gain a desired change in their circumstances, and (2) they seek active association with relatively like-minded persons to gain relief from their aggrieved state.

These two characteristics can be seen among protest participants over time and in different locales. In the 1960s civil rights movements in the United States, leading activists—including blacks, Hispanics, Native Americans, and women—expressed a strong sense of unequal treatment and opportunity while associating with and supporting activists to achieve equal opportunities in schools, jobs, elected offices, and other social settings. College students, the most active participants in the civil rights movement, could not generally be characterized in these minority status terms. Yet, they were not yet an established part of the economic and political order being challenged and were in a position to be critical of that order. Other participant supporters, such as labor unions, selected corporate leaders, and religiously motivated persons, often saw protest-related change needed in terms of their own long-term interests and worked either to help the civil rights movement succeed or to preempt or coopt it. . . .

The methods employed by protest participants and leaders tend to reflect a lack of institutionalized power. When such institutionalized power is available, it can be exercised to redress grievances without resorting to mass protests. . . .

Methods of protest are related to prospects of success and levels of frustration. When a protest movement or a countermovement has broad public support and is likely to receive a positive response from targeted authorities, protest activities are likely to be peaceful and accepted by such authorities. Such is the case with pro-choice protest on the abortion issue; protest for clean air; and protest in support of Christian, Jewish, and other minority religious status groups in the [former] Soviet Union. All these protest activities have relatively broad American support, even when they experience a minority activist opposition.

Nonlegitimate and Violent Protest Strategies

A variety of nonlegitimate strategies [i.e., not accepted by authorities as legitimate forms of protest] are used when protest movements address issues and involve participants with relatively little initial public support and active opposition. One such nonlegitimate strategy is [Indian nationalist leader Mohandas] Gandhi's nonviolent protest confrontation with British authorities in India. Adapted by Martin Luther King, Jr., and most other black civil rights protest leaders in the 1950s and early 1960s, the strategy of nonviolence was designed to call general public attention in a nonthreatening manner to perceived injustices experienced by blacks. With such techniques as sit-ins at racially segregated lunch counters and boycotts of segregated public buses, this nonviolent method generated conflict by breaking down established social practices. The aim of such nonviolent methods is to advance conflict resolution by negotiating a change in practices that produced the protest. A particularly famous case is the 1955 Montgomery, Alabama, bus boycott, which was one of several major precipitants of the national black-led civil rights movement.

Other, violent forms of protest include both planned strategies and unplanned spontaneous crowd action. In either case such activity tends to be perceived by authorities and their supporters as disorderly and lawless mob behavior. Masses of protest

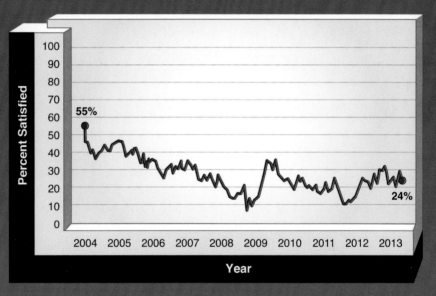

Percent of Americans Satisfied with the Way Things Are Going in United States, 2004–2013

Americans were asked by the Gallup polling organization, "In general, are you satisfied or dissatisfied with the way things are going in the United States at this time?" Between 2004 and 2013 satisfaction levels have declined significantly, indicating a potential for increased social protest.

55%

24%

Percent Satisfied

2004 2005 2006 2007 2008 2009 2010 2011 2012 2013

Year

Taken from: Frank Newport. "U.S. Satisfaction Drops to 24% in May." Gallup Politics, May 14, 2013.
www.gallup.com/poll/162512/satisfaction-drops-may.aspx.

participants are likely to be drawn to violent action when the general perception . . . develops that redress of felt grievances is believed to be unattainable either in normal conditions before protest activation or by peaceful means. The history of violent protest is extensive in many societies, as exemplified by the forcible occupation of farms and fields by landless French peasants in the eighteenth century, American attacks on British possessions and military posts prior to the Declaration of Independence, and bread riots by Russian urban dwellers in World War I. The particular centuries-long history of violent protest movements in

American society was documented in [the] context of the urban race riots and anti–Vietnam War protest in the 1960s. . . .

Violent protests usually concern specific issues such as taxes, conscription into the military, and food shortages, issues that are confined to particular situations and times. Although these types of protest do not evolve into major social movements, they may have severe and immediate consequences. In 1863, for instance, during the Civil War, Irish Catholics protested what they perceived as the unfair nature of the military draft in New York City. This protest left several hundred dead. Likewise, many college students in the late 1960s and the early 1970s revolted against the draft during the unpopular Vietnam War, and the results included loss of student lives at Kent State University [where four unarmed students were killed and nine were wounded by Ohio National Guardsmen]. Unplanned violence may also be a form of protest. As reported by the National Advisory Commission on Civil Disorders and other research on over two dozen urban racial riots in the 1960s in the United States, these riots, which resulted in over a hundred deaths and over $100 million in property damage, were disorganized extensions of the black civil rights movement. . . .

Overall, protest movements are more frequent in societies that legitimize the right of protest. In such societies, social conflict generated by protest movements is often functional in resolving conflict over issues between challenging and target groups. Still, urban and campus riots of the 1960s illustrate that formal rights of protest do not deter democratic authorities and their public supporters from responding with police force or from beginning a countermovement. Authoritarian societies may experience fewer protest movements, but when they do occur, such movements are far more likely to be intense and to have the potential for massive social movements designed to transform the society. This could be seen in widely disparate societies, including most eastern European nations and the Soviet Union, El Salvador, Nicaragua, South Africa, Iran, and mainland China.

Consequences of Protest Movements

Given the long and continuing history of protest movements, there has been growing interest in the long-term consequences of such movements. . . .

Successful or unsuccessful in the short or the long term, protest movements are periodically a part of social change at local, national, and global levels. . . . In the United States and other modern mass urban societies, the long-term trend has been for protest movements to become more professionalized with increased mobilization of resources to more effectively challenge entrenched interests. Modern communication systems, global economic interdependence, and economical movement of masses of people over great distances assures that protest movements of the future will increasingly be characterized by a combination of ideas, people, and organization across all these areas of social life.

TWO

Nonviolent Protest Is the Only Effective Means of Protest

Bryan Farrell

Bryan Farrell is a New York–based writer, covering topics such as climate change, militarism, and foreign policy. In the following viewpoint Farrell argues that violence has no place in political protests because it consistently undermines the goals the protest is attempting to achieve. He describes how a small group of anarchists at a protest in Toronto, Ontario, Canada, in 2010 broke off from the main group of peaceful protesters and started breaking store windows and burning police cars. The result was a massive police crackdown and many arrests. He claims that such tactics frighten the public and discredit the protest and whatever message it is trying to convey. According to the author, nonviolent protest is much more likely to make progress in achieving its aims. Farrell says nonviolent protest is actually composed of many different tactics, noting that author Gene Sharp describes 198 different nonviolent tactics in his book *Waging Nonviolent Struggle*.

During Saturday's [June 27, 2010] nonviolent protest of about 5,000 activists outside the conference center in downtown Toronto [Ontario, Canada], where leaders of the G20 [the top twenty world economies] were meeting, several hundred masked figures dressed in black broke away and started torching police cars and smashing store fronts. Not only did this steal the attention away from the peaceful protesters, but it got a lot of them hurt and arrested. By the end of the day's events, the police had beaten activists and journalists, fired tear gas and rubber bullets, and arrested more than 560 people.

Just about anyone following the G20 [summit conference] could have seen this coming. In the weeks before, Canada was busy building what [the British newspaper] *The Guardian* called "the toughest security cordon in the history of the summit," spending an estimated $1 billion . . . and bringing in 19,000 police officers. So, clearly it was ready to use them. But more importantly, why was it so ready to use them?

Violent Tactics Render Protest Ineffective

Some might point to the threat of vandalism promised by a group of Ontario anarchists a month before the summit. In a message to its members, the Southern Ontario Anarchist Resistance (SOAR) announced its plan to stage "militant protests" and to "humiliate the security apparatus" by using "a variety of tactics"— a common phrase used by anarchists who perceive nonviolent action as ineffective. But as is so often the case, such dismissal stems from a complete lack of knowledge as to the dynamics of nonviolent action.

In what sounds like a reasonable appeal, SOAR told its members, "Respect for diversity of tactics also means not smashing things while we're part of the labour child-friendly march, and remembering that although we might think certain tactics are pointless/annoying, we should not needlessly antagonize those people."

What these anarchists don't seem to realize is that nonviolent campaigns lose their power and are generally rendered pointless when they are associated with people who act violently.

This is why governments are always eager to paint their critics as violent, and sometimes, as police in Quebec did two years ago [in 2008], plant saboteurs to incite violence. In fact, there's been some speculation that the security forces in Toronto encouraged acts of destruction. In regards to the three police cars that were set on fire, *The Guardian* wrote:

Questions are being asked as to why the police chose to drive the vehicles into the middle of a group of protesters and then abandon them, and why there was no attempt to put out the flames until the nation's media had been given time to record the scenes for broadcast around the world.

A "Variety of Tactics"

If this is true, it doesn't really say much for SOAR and the effectiveness of its "variety of tactics" approach. It suggests that they are considered more of a convenient pawn than a serious threat. In fact, the real threat is a strong nonviolent movement able to appeal to the public by exposing the illegitimacy of the G20. It's only on the surface that the security apparatus is able to justify a massive crackdown based on threats of vandalism. No megacorporation is facing serious existential danger because of some smashed windows.

Of course, this anarchist offshoot has argued the contrary, saying that since mass audiences "generally dismiss every form of direct action and every radical cause" (a claim that is not supported), there isn't any utility in trying to win the public over to a given cause. Therefore, the point of their destructive action is to "put people on notice that there exists active insurrectionary resistance, right here in the belly of the beast"—an explanation that could ironically apply to a nonviolent campaign as well.

Another point of contention that should be noted is that SOAR and other anarchists like them do not view themselves as violent. As one masked protester told the *Toronto Star* newspaper: "This isn't violence. This is vandalism against violent corporations. We did not hurt anybody. [The corporations] are the ones hurting people."

Unfortunately, this rings as a rather naive, if not even disingenuous, statement. There are differing views on whether or not vandalism is a form of violence, and while there's no doubt it pales

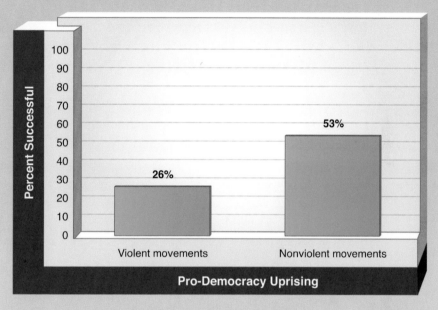

Success Rates of Violent and Nonviolent Pro-Democracy Uprisings

A study by Maria J. Stephan and Erica Chenoweth of 323 major pro-democracy movements that have taken place since 1900 found that nonviolent movements had a much higher success rate than violent ones.

Percent Successful

53%

26%

Violent movements   Nonviolent movements

Pro-Democracy Uprising

Taken from: Maria J. Stephan and Erica Chenoweth. "Why Civil Resistance Works: The Strategic Logic of Nonviolent Conflict." *International Security,* vol. 33, no. 1 (Summer 2008), pp. 7–44. http://belfercenter.ksg.harvard.edu/files /IS3301_pp007–044_Stephan_Chenoweth.pdf.

in comparison to the violence corporations engage in every day, it does scare people and furthermore leads to a string of unintended consequences.

Peaceful Protest Produces Better Results

In Toronto, it led to the passage of draconian laws. . . . At least one family had their home mistakenly broken into by gun-brandishing police officers. Also, "non-lethal" weapons, such as tear gas, were used for the first time ever on the public citizenry of Toronto.

Okanagan Mission Secondary School

Anarchists engaged in vandalism may continue to dismiss the role they play in the perpetuation of violence, but they will do so at their own peril. There is no evidence of their tactics working toward any kind of positive change.

Looking back on the World Trade Organization [WTO] protests in Seattle [Washington] 10 years ago [1999], we do not hear anyone applauding the work of those who smashed windows. If anything it's taken 10 years to overcome those images and get people to recognize that Seattle was a largely nonviolent campaign that effectively shut down the WTO for years to come.

Protesters stand face-to-face with police officers at the 2010 Toronto G20 summit.

Perhaps the most encouraging result of the aftermath was that Seattle's police chief not only apologized to the peaceful protesters but also came around to seeing their perspective and has become a critic of globalization. If there's any chance of that happening again, it's going to be through undisturbed nonviolent action.

Nonviolent Protesters Have Room for Improvement

None of this is to say, however, that the nonviolent protesters in Toronto are blameless for the general dismissal of their action. They bear responsibility for not figuring out a way to distinguish themselves from the anarchist vandals. Nearly every anti-globalization demonstration is hijacked by this group, and nonviolent activists should have a plan for dealing with them by now.

Finally, G20 activists have done a poor job of making their demands known. The array of groups and issues present at G20 demonstrations confuses the public, and rather than try to figure out how all the issues are connected, they just write everyone off as a bunch of misfits and societal castoffs.

The good news is that in the world of nonviolence, these are surmountable problems. Nonviolence isn't the one tactic anarchists make it out to be. In his book *Waging Nonviolent Struggle*, Gene Sharp identified 198 methods of nonviolent action. If G20 activists can isolate the ones that aren't working for them and employ new ones, perhaps the next demonstration will close the gap between the frustrated anarchists and the ignored peaceful protesters.

THREE

Direct Action, Including Violence, Is Sometimes Necessary to Effect Change

Phil Dickens

Phil Dickens is an anarchist, antifascist, and trade-union activist from Liverpool, England. In the following viewpoint he argues that positive change in society does not come about because a ruling class decides to benevolently bestow it upon the masses, or because of polite, orderly protests; rather, it takes much more direct and often criminal and/or violent actions on the part of protesters to create real and lasting change. He gives a number of examples throughout history, including the Haymarket massacre of 1886 in Chicago, in which workers demanded and eventually won the right to an eight-hour workday; in that movement a series of strikes was met with police brutality, a bomb was thrown at police, and many protesters were killed. Ultimately the movement prevailed. Dickens asserts that change only happens when people stand up and demand concessions from those who rule society.

Phil Dickens, "In Support of Direct Action," *Property Is Theft!* (blog), June 6, 2009. www.propertyistheft.wordpress.com. Reproduced by permission.

In the popular imagination, the term "direct action" conjures up images of violence and chaos. Masked thugs rampaging the streets, battling with the police, spraying graffiti on walls, throwing eggs, bricks. Smashed windows, social disorder, and impotent alarms caterwauling into the night.

But, as with all that offers a challenge to the ruling class and the status quo, the public perception is wildly different from the reality.

I argue that, far from sowing the seeds of disorder, direct action—in *all* its forms—is the precise reason that we enjoy the (limited) freedoms we do today. Moreover, that it remains the most effective way of forcing positive societal changes from the ruling classes.

Defining Direct Action

In order to make a positive argument in favour of direct action, we must first understand precisely what it is. As a useful starting point, Wikipedia defines the term thus:

> Direct action is politically motivated activity undertaken by individuals, groups, or governments to achieve political goals outside of normal social/political channels. Direct action can include nonviolent and violent activities which target persons, groups, or property deemed offensive to the direct action participant. Examples of nonviolent direct action include strikes, workplace occupations, sit-ins, and graffiti. Violent direct actions include sabotage, vandalism, assault, and murder. By contrast, grassroots organizing, electoral politics, diplomacy and negotiation or arbitration does not constitute direct action. Direct actions are sometimes a form of civil disobedience, but some (such as strikes) do not always violate criminal law.

The aim of direct action is to draw attention to, and support for, an action or position at a grassroots level. Its purpose is to force its cause onto the agenda and bring about change, outside of the normal bureaucratic and political channels which by design bar all interests unpalatable to ruling elites.

The best way, perhaps, to explain this concept fully is by providing select examples and listing their achievements.

Direct Action and Its Achievements in History

As alluded earlier, direct action is responsible for all of the freedoms that we enjoy today. Society has not advanced because a benevolent ruling class has granted the masses generous concessions out of the goodness of its heart, not because of passive petitioning and asking politely if we might, please, have better conditions. Rather, even the tiniest concession of liberty by those in power is begrudging, forced from them by revolutionary actions and large-scale disobedience by the masses, and remains under constant threat of being rolled back as long as a ruling class exists.

Direct action by the peasantry, the workers, or the popular masses has won us everything from the eight-hour day and the right to join a trade union to universal suffrage and basic freedom of speech. As a demonstration of this, I will run through a few examples.

The Haymarket Massacre

On 1st May, 1886, Chicago's working class—with the city's anarchist movement at the fore—began a series of strike actions in support of the American Federation of Labor's resolution that "eight hours shall constitute a legal day's labour from and after May 1st, 1886." They came to a head on May 3rd when police assaulted and shot at marchers.

In response, anarchist August Spies organised a demonstration on May 4th in Haymarket Square against the attacks. When police moved in to forcibly disperse the protesters, a bomb was thrown at them. They responded with gunfire, mass slaughter, and the rounding up of the eight ringleaders. Four of them—including August Spies—were executed.

Libcom [a libertarian communist website] sums up the aftermath of the executions:

> 600,000 working people turned out for their funeral. The campaign to free Neebe, Schwab and Fielden [the surviv-

ing Haymarket anarchists] continued. On June 26th 1893 Governor [John P.] Altgeld set them free. He made it clear he was not granting the pardon because he thought the men had suffered enough, but because they were innocent of the crime for which they had been tried. They and the hanged men had been the victims of "hysteria, packed juries and a biased judge."

The authorities believed at the time of the trial that such persecution would break the back of the eight-hour movement. Indeed, evidence later came to light that the bomb may have been thrown by a police agent working for Captain [John] Bonfield, as part of a conspiracy involving certain steel bosses to discredit the labour movement.

When Spies addressed the court after he had been sentenced to die, he was confident that this conspiracy would not succeed:

"If you think that by hanging us you can stamp out the labour movement . . . the movement from which the downtrodden millions, the millions who toil in misery and want, expect salvation—if this is your opinion, then hang us! Here you will tread on a spark, but there and there, behind you—and in front of you, and everywhere, flames blaze up. It is a subterranean fire. You cannot put it out."

As a result of the struggle and sacrifice of men like Spies, workers in the west now enjoy the right to work no more than eight hours per day. The struggle continues elsewhere, in the Haymarket tradition, but there can be no doubt that the direct action of that day in 1886 bears prime responsibility for any enjoyment of eight-hour days in the present.

The Suffragette Movement

Without a doubt, the reason that women have the vote today is because of the women whom the *New York Times* of November 18, 1906 described as "a handful of violent cranks." The paper describes how the movement was "making a deliberate and well-

An illustration depicts the anarchist Haymarket riot and massacre on May 4, 1886, in Chicago.

organized attempt to shame and scare Parliament into granting votes to women." "They came to the conclusion that the cause of woman suffrage [*sic*] would be best achieved were the Suffragists to make themselves as unpleasant as possible to the authorities."

In this assumption, they were proven right. As even the *Times* article concedes, twelve years before the Representation of the People Act 1918, "the Suffragettes have done more in the last few weeks to obtain victory for their cause than the old-fashioned Suffragists [an earlier, more peaceful form of the movement] succeeded in accomplishing in many years."

The Civil Rights Movement

On 1st December 1955, a black woman refused to give up her seat on a bus for a white passenger. [Seamstress] Rosa Parks' action drew greater attention to the plight of blacks as second class citizens in the United States and inspired the Montgomery Bus Boycott, the spark that lit the tinder of the African-American Civil Rights Movement.

The Bus Boycott was only the first in a broad campaign of direct action. In 1960, sit-ins at lunch counters, parks, beaches, libraries, theaters, museums, and other public places forced the issue of segregationist policies onto the public agenda. The following year, in the face of massive violence from the Ku Klux Klan [KKK] and state collaborators, activists engaged in "Freedom Rides" aimed at integrating seating patterns and desegregating bus terminals, including restrooms and water fountains, in the Deep South.

After the Freedom Rides, and again in the face of KKK and state repression, there was a massive drive to organise and register black voters in Mississippi. After a swathe of desegregation and integrationist campaigns, 1963 saw the March on Washington for Jobs and Freedom. This massive protest march, comprised of all of the major civil rights organizations, the more progressive wing of the labor movement, and other liberal organizations as well as black civil rights groups, aimed at pushing for "meaningful civil rights laws, a massive federal works program, full and fair employment, decent housing, the right to vote, and adequate integrated education."

The above is just a snapshot of the direct action that took place in support of black civil rights. Activists were arrested and jailed, beaten by police and racist groups alike, took part in marches, sat down and refused to move, occupied buildings and places of business, and forcibly upset the double standards of the status quo. With the Civil Rights Act of 1964, the National Voting Rights Act of 1965, and visible change to the very psyche of the United States, the achievements of the movement are undeniable.

Direct Action Today

Today [in 2009], the tradition of direct action continues apace. To give just a few examples, anarchists in Greece are engaged in running battles with neo-fascist paramilitary groups and their police collaborators, anti-deportation activists continually engage in blockades protesting illegal detention and mass deportation, auto workers in Korea occupied their place of work in protest at proposed job losses, and parents in Lewisham [a district in London, England] have occupied Lewisham bridge primary school in protest over its closure. One might also cite the Camp for Climate Action and the No Borders Camp in Calais [France] as examples of ongoing direct action aimed at highlighting broader issues.

However, almost without exception, direct action is derided as "counterproductive," a "mere distraction," "hooliganism," "out of touch with the real world," and even "terroristic." Authoritarians and "moderates" . . . don't like it for the simple reason that it upsets the status quo.

But that is precisely the point.

If all protest was of the "legal" and "orderly" type—i.e. confined to cordoned-off "free speech zones," drowned in police presence, unseen, and unheard—then nothing would ever be accomplished. Indeed, we might even begin to move backwards. Progress is what happens when ordinary people take to the streets en massé and force as much concession from the ruling classes as possible. Societal advance is the result of ever more layers of power being stripped from the state and capital.

During the Spanish Revolution [1936], [anarchist militant] Buenaventura Durruti Dumange said this:

> It is we the workers who built these palaces and cities here in Spain and in America and everywhere. We, the workers, can build others to take their place. And better ones! We are not in the least afraid of ruins. We are going to inherit the earth; there is not the slightest doubt about that. The bourgeoisie [middle class] might blast and ruin its own world before it leaves the stage of history. We carry a new world here, in our hearts. That world is growing this minute.

The only thing that stops this being true is our submission. When those in power cannot use the brutal force exacted

against the Haymarket rioters, it locks us up in pens and calls it "free speech," and the hounds of the media print lie after lie after lie. Whatever form suppression takes, it must be resisted. "Moderation" is the admission that you have no desire to see your goals and visions come to pass. Direct action is the only guaranteed agent of progressive change in our society.

Waiting on the benevolence of those above will achieve nothing. Only direct action can force through positive change. If we are to see a better world, then it is our duty to disobey.

FOUR

Comedy and Street Theater Are Effective Protest Tactics

Wayne Grytting

Wayne Grytting is a former teacher in Seattle Washington, and the author of *American Newspeak: The Mangling of Meaning for Power and Profit.* In the following viewpoint Grytting asserts that nonviolent protests around the world have in recent years increasingly taken up absurd and theatrical strategies to further their causes. The author gives numerous examples of such protests, such as labor unions in Chile organizing a "national day of slow movement" to avoid a violent confrontation with police that would likely have occurred if they had staged a conventional strike. Another example is a protest in 2011 in the United States called "Corporate Zombie Day," in which protesters dressed up as zombies and lurched around chanting "I smell money." According to Grytting, such tactics can be effective by undermining authorities' ability to counter the demonstrations and by building confidence in protesters through fun activities that help create a sense of community.

On October 3rd [2011], protesters at Occupy Wall Street failed to march. Instead they clumsily lurched. With white painted faces, glazed looks and dollar bills hanging out of some mouths, protesters chanted "I smell money, I smell money. . . ."

Wayne Grytting, "Gandhi Meets Monty Python: The Comedic Turn in Nonviolent Tactics," *Waging Nonviolence*, October 28, 2011. www.wagingnonviolence.org. Copyright © 2011 by Waging Nonviolence. All rights reserved. Reproduced by permission.

It was Corporate Zombie Day. Scenes like this and the sight of Guy Fawkes masks [in the likeness of the protester who planned to retake the English throne for Catholics in 1605], clown suits, drumming circles and surrealistic posters all over the country have left many commentators scratching their heads. Is this protest or carnival? Maybe we should tell them. There's been a sea change in the protest industry.

"A worldwide shift in revolutionary tactics is underway right now that bodes well for the future," proclaims *Adbusters*, the initiators of Occupy Wall Street. A key part of this re-channeling of tactics has been a move away from both angry protests or passive waiting-to-be-clubbed-by-police-batons to age old carnival-style antics. A festive atmosphere has reigned supreme in all of the successful pro-democracy uprisings of the past two decades. In Poland, Serbia, Georgia, Ukraine, Tunisia and Egypt, music and humor were everywhere. Why?

Countering Fear with Humor

Musically, Eastern European rallies were powered by punk rock bands while in the Arab Spring [widespread protests in Middle East], "hip-hop has become the rhythm of the resistance," writes author Robin Wright. Tahrir Square [in Cairo, Egypt], says journalist Sarah Carr, "was essentially a comedy explosion." Tunisia was "a pioneer in revolution and now it's at the forefront in comic expression," proclaims the voice of Captain Khuzba, the masked cartoon hero who fought Tunisia's secret police armed with a loaf of French bread. In Serbia's pro-democracy movement in 2000, Srdja Popovic, a leader of Otpor ("Resistance") reports, "Everything we did had a dosage of humor."

Otpor is the organization credited with forging the nonviolent tactics used in the Arab Spring and earlier pro-democracy movements in Georgia and Ukraine. Founded in 1998 following a period of failed demonstrations by a small ragged group of twenty-somethings, it had within two years built a movement that overthrew Serbia's dictator Slobodan Milosevic. Otpor learned early that humor could be a gigantic ice breaker, cutting through citizen's fear and apathy and "turning oppression upside down." They fine tuned the art of comedic resistance, added modern marketing techniques and the strategic framework provided by [influential pioneer of nonviolent protest] Gene Sharp.

The starting point for Sharp in *From Dictatorship to Democracy* is a recognition that, "The common error of past improvised political defiance campaigns is the reliance on only one or two methods, such as strikes and mass demonstrations." His remedy was a heavy dosage of "low-risk, confidence-building actions." Street theater and under-the-radar comic protests. Following this path, Mykhailo Svystovych, of Ukraine's youth movement group Pora ("It's Time") recalls: "We didn't do rallies with speakers, we did theatrical events." The massive rallies we viewed on TV—this was the final chapter prepared by years of small guerrilla incursions.

Who were Otpor's heroes? In interviews they list names we might expect: [Indian nationalist leader Mohandas] Gandhi, [African American civil rights leader] Martin Luther King Jr., and an unexpected source: [British comedy troupe] *Monty Python's Flying Circus*.

Examples of Humorous Protests

Stop the presses. What? How did those clowns sneak into the club? What is it about Monty Python–style humor that lends itself to deposing tyrannies? Let's look closely at the exact laughter-creating tactics developed in these movements so you can judge for yourself—and maybe add to your own resume. Fortunately, excellent stories have been collected by authors Tina Rosenberg ("Revolution U"), Patrick Kearny (*A Carnival of Revolution*), Matthew Collin (*The Time of the Rebels*) and video producer Steven York (*A Force More Powerful*).

1. Flying Under the Radar

Dictators typically outlaw protest marches and give their security forces carte blanche to bash heads. In South Africa, blacks "solved" the problem by assembling large gatherings at funerals, the one kind of gathering the Apartheid government was not ready to ban. How could the deceased help it if she or he had

© S. Harris/www.CartoonStock.com.

tens of thousands of friends who wanted to mourn and follow the hearse through town? In Serbia, Otpor developed a tactic of "flash" protests, introducing a game called "Arrest the Traffic Lights." People would mob street intersections and simply jump up and down while the walk lights were green. When the light changed they'd carefully obey the law and disperse only to resume their protest when the light said "go" again.

In Chile in 1983 labor unions made plans for their first test of [President Augusto] Pinochet after 10 years of violent repression. Copper miners about to go on strike observed the large number of soldiers assembling by their mines and swiftly changed tactics. Instead of a strike, they called for a national day of slow movement. All over Chile, people simply drove, walked or worked in slow motion to express their solidarity. Later they banged on pots and pans at exactly 8PM. How do you arrest slow walkers or pot bangers? It's a massive clown routine worthy of [French mime] Marcel Marceau. How could you not smile at your fellow slow motion actors? After that the ice was broken and an irresistible wave of protests began.

2. Obedience Parody

If protests against a government are being discouraged, and you feel a need to walk with a large group, you can always choose to march in "support" of the government. So Otpor paraded "for" Milosevic's socialist party, but did so with a small herd of sheep with signs around their necks announcing "We support the Socialist Party." In the Ukraine, student members of Pora ("It's Time") fought against the usurped election of their local tyrant named [Viktor] Yanukovych. He had a prison record so Pora members dressed up in prison uniforms and campaigned for him in the main streets of Kiev, Ukraine's capital. In Egypt, activists helped government officials by setting up Facebook pages for them and Twitter accounts so they could spread their messages. One official's favorite activities were listed for him as: "Kicking ass, taking names, and wearing decorations with more colors than you can find in a pack of Skittles."

In Poland in 1987, a group of "socialist surrealists" called the Orange Alternative . . . produced parodies of official events. On one April Fool's Day they marched to the central square in Wroclaw to express their love of the government through a voluntary work day. Armed with mops and toothbrushes—which was very inefficient, I might add—they proceeded to clean up the square while singing socialist labor songs and dressing up like ideal workers from old Stalinist movies of the 1930s. Police again confronted the problem—what can you arrest them for? Cleaning up the square is a crime? Acting as fools gained protesters immunity from repression and a strengthened community of smiling co-conspirators.

3. Therapeutic Pies in the Face

If moving slowly together can help create community, imagine what collectively throwing a pie in the face of a dictator can be like. Otpor, in their most famous actions, brought out barrels with Milosevic's picture on it and let people hit it with a stick for only one dinar. Those who were unemployed because of Milosevic could hit it twice for free. The police only looked ridiculous when they stepped in to, in the words of Otpor, "arrest" the barrel. Pictures of the "arrest" would soon be posted on the

Internet. In [the former Soviet republic of] Georgia in 2003, the group Kmara ("Enough") created large banners where passersby could take photos of themselves flushing their president, Eduard Shevardnadze, down the toilet. In Ukraine, by 2004 the action had moved to the Internet where citizens could throw eggs at their soon-to-be-deposed leader Yanukovych, who had famously overreacted to a real egg throwing incident.

What is hitting a picture of a dictator but a version of the dunk tank? These actions go back to centuries-old carnival traditions of ridiculing the high and mighty. They crop up in movement after movement because they meet very basic needs. Throwing a pie at authority can be a low-risk participatory event with an appreciative community cheering one on. It's not lazily watching [political satirist and anchor of *The Daily Show*] Jon Stewart on TV—it's physical action against authority, a physical break with patterns of passivity and isolation, a nonviolent rechanneling of simmering anger.

4. *Idiocy Rising to the Top*

Much of the humor of movements requires faith, a conviction that if you just set the table, the other side's idiocy will provide all the humor necessary. For example, Otpor had their offices raided and computers hauled away. Knowing they had an informer "assisting" their activities, they put out the word they would be bringing in a load of new computer equipment. At the "secret" time trucks pulled up with heavy looking boxes. While laboring to lift these loads, the police intervened, only to discover all the boxes were empty. The story, with photos, went viral.

When Serbia's government leveled charges that Otpor was a foreign-paid terrorist organization, Otpor took flatbed trucks and megaphones to the streets to denounce and expose the "terrorists" in their midst. They brought 17 and 18-year-old "terrorist" students in front of the public and grilled them about their activities. Similarly, in Egypt, when the government officials denounced the protesters for serving "foreign agendas," young people showed up at Tahrir Square with plain blank notebooks, complaining they'd left their foreign agendas at home.

5. Absurdity Squared

Community organizing guru Saul Alinsky's famous *Rules for Radicals* #3 states: "Whenever possible, go outside the experience of the enemy." Or any forms of rationality they might ever recognize. We enter here into pure Monty Python territory. Otpor, for example, would hold fake soccer games in the streets complete with uniformed referees and an imaginary soccer ball. Or they would hold parades in ridiculous fancy dress with no protest slogans, or gaily deliver cookies and flowers to police stations.

In Serbia's pro-democracy movement in 2000, Srdja Popovic (pictured), a leader of Otpor ("Resistance"), reports, "Everything we did had a dosage of humor."

My favorite example is from the Orange Alternative in Poland. After the group carefully spray painted graffiti around Wroclaw, the police would come by and paint it over with white paint. This would leave unsightly white splotches on building walls. Instead of posting yet more graffiti, the activists took red paint and turned the splotches into elves. . . . As more and more red elves appeared, this morphed into a demonstration where thousands dressed up in red and marched chanting "Elves are real!"

American activists will recognize most of the elements of the festive model. Certainly the street theater of the AIDS Coalition to Unleash Power (ACT UP) or "Billionaires for Bush" [satirizing President George W. Bush for, in their view, serving the interests of the wealthy] anticipates much of the spirit of the pro-democracy movements. But what stands out in the new movements is the integration of the class clowns with the nerds, of spontaneity with nonviolent discipline. Traditionally people attracted to festive protests, group hugs and consensus decision making have been too laid back to organize effectively. The successful pro-democracy groups have managed to combine these elements with a caffeinated backbone of organizers who make the trains run on time and know when to shift gears. . . .

Monty Python–style humor is rooted in centuries-old carnival traditions which, as Russian scholar Mikhail Bakhtin has so brilliantly taught us, emphasize that all of us are fools and clowns just waiting to slip on banana peels. It has a humility that cuts through any vestiges of elitism or know-it-all political correctness.

Carnival represents the joyful life that stands as the total opposite of the zombie-like death of corporate rule. It's what I believe allowed Otpor and other pro-democracy groups of twenty-somethings to bridge age and cultural gaps and build powerful movements.

Occupy Wall Street is a bold "experiment in truth," which my stock analysts tell me should lead to a bull market in protests. Let's keep a smile on it.

FIVE

Theatrical Confrontation Is No Longer an Effective Protest Tactic

Chez Pazienza

Chez Pazienza is a journalist, a TV news producer and editor of *The Daily Banter* website. In the following viewpoint he argues that the kind of protest tactics once effectively used by the baby boomer generation that came of age in the 1960s and 1970s do not work very well in the twenty-first century. According to the author, the use of shocking theatricality, humor, and outrageous individuality worked so well back then because at the time, most people were very conformist and consequently were shocked by such displays. However, in the modern era that kind of individualism is no longer even possible because the media have completely appropriated and commercialized all expressions of defiance or rebellion, thus rendering non-conformity meaningless. Pazienza suggests that if people want to protest against modern issues like drone warfare, they need to come up with more-effective protest tactics that better suit the modern era.

I've said this sort of thing before many times. [Journalist] Matt Taibbi's said it. [Comedian] David Cross does an entire bit about it. But no matter how often it's repeated, there are still those out there on the left who live in their own little . . . bubble and don't seem to get something: the 60s are over and continuing to protest like it's 1967 will get you absolutely nowhere in the year 2013. Yes, it'll grab you a little attention, but ultimately not the kind you want. It's an ineffective model of activism in the new millennium and the predisposition to fall back on it needs to be shelved once and for all.

Yesterday [February 7, 2013], in a scene as predictable as it was pointless, members of [antiwar protest group] Code Pink crashed the confirmation hearing of CIA [Central Intelligence Agency] chief nominee John Brennan. They stood up with their posters emblazoned with pithy cracks like "Don't Drone Me, Bro!" waved hands that they'd painted pink, and shouted at the top of their lungs about how Brennan was a murderer and how they stood for mothers who'd lost loved ones overseas in America's drone campaign against [terrorist organization] Al Qaeda. One of them even brandished some kind of puppet or doll that I guess was supposed to be a baby. They did this over and over again until [US senator] Dianne Feinstein had to finally clear the room, eventually allowing many back in but exiling the Code Pink people to the arms of waiting reporters outside, where at least this time, as far as I know, they did their histrionic interviews without the assistance of the giant papier-mâché effigy of Brennan they brought to the White House last month [January 2013].

Audacious Individuality Is No Longer Shocking

I made it clear yesterday that while I acknowledge the dangers of a continued drone war overseas and certainly see how the issue of collateral damage on the ground and secret kill lists here at home could prompt some serious discussion, I personally don't have it in me to get so worked up over any of it that I feel the need to take

The Tea Party employed the tactics of ridicule in a 2012 protest against President Barack Obama's health care plan, including theatrics and costumes, which the viewpoint author argues are no longer an effective protest strategy as they were in the more conformist 1960s.

to the streets. That said, this is America and there isn't a thing wrong with voicing your opinion on the subject of how the U.S. has been prosecuting the so-called "war on terror." The thing is, if it infuriates you and you feel the need to work toward changing it or stopping it altogether, you're going to want a plan for making your views heard in a way that's potent and that has some hope of accomplishing what you set out to.

In the late 1960s, the way to do that was by making a lot of very loud noise and turning almost every protest into a [Japanese] Kabuki theater–style spectacle. This worked because we were living in a time when the masses were actually terrified of individuality; it was considered a serious threat to the established order, one that had already begun to upend that order, and so any expression of it not only got attention, it got results.

But the rules have changed over the years. Now not only is individualism and public outrage not shocking or dangerous, it's an almost comical anachronism. As I've said before, there is no individualism these days. Nothing truly audacious can stand in our culture, not when our culture has become so monstrously adept at assimilating all forms of rebellion until they become completely meaningless and utterly impotent. Prepackaged, homogenized non-conformity is as close as your local Hot Topic. Agitation is fashion. Defiance is a slogan. Insurrection is product placement. The revolution is not only televised, it can be DVRed and enjoyed at your convenience.

More Up-to-Date Tactics Are Needed

When the Code Pink troops stand up and shout down a confirmation hearing before the guy at the center of it really even has a chance to start speaking—Brennan was just thanking *his wife* when the hell started being raised—and produce puppets and pink hands in the process they're not only creating a cacophonous mess, they're providing endless fodder for the idiots at [conservative] Fox News, who get to smirk patronizingly and present it as red meat to their audience of bitter old people. It's left-wing agitators just being left-wing agitators—and what's more, it barely even gets the point at hand across. Yeah, you made a statement, but who cares if no one can figure out the details of what that statement is besides your not wanting to be "droned, bro?" You made news, but to what end?

By the way, there's an irony to the fact that the Tea Party right employed the very same kinds of tactics a couple of years back, unwittingly adopting the ridiculous protest model of its enemy,

Public Support for Occupy Movement Aims and Tactics, December 7–11, 2011

The Occupy movement that took place in the United States and around the world in 2011 used controversial and theatrical tactics that were in some ways reminiscent of the protests of the 1960s. According to a Pew Research Center poll in December 2011, agreement with the goals of the Occupy movement was much higher than support for the tactics used.

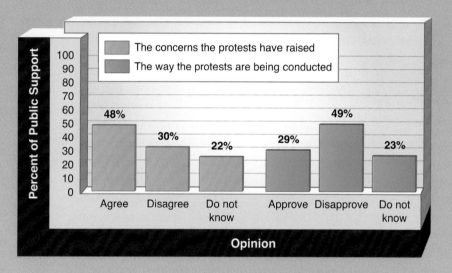

Taken from: Chris Bowers. "New Poll Shows Occupy Wall Street Support Growing, Public Discontent with Congress at Record Levels." *Daily Kos*, December 15, 2011. www.dailykos.com/story/2011/12/15/1045683/-new-poll-shows-Occupy -Wall-Street-support-growing-public-discontet-with-Congress-at-record-levels.

right down to the silly costumes, unfunny "comic" signs and unfocused rage. These antics gave their political adversaries the same kind of thrill up their spines that the right gets from watching those kooky, moonbat lefties ranting about injustice while wearing robot suits. (As David Cross says, "Another silver robot for peace!") There are so many new outlets and models for effective protest these days—the kind of thing that can capture attention without thoroughly alienating those whose views you want to change and making yourselves look like easily dismissible clowns in the process—that there's no excuse for not availing yourself of them and choosing instead to stubbornly trudge on with the worn-out [Baby] Boomer playbook.

If you believe the new technology of killer drones and the potential judicial overreach in using them are a fact of American life in the year 2013 that you simply can't tolerate, you might want to stop looking back to a time before either of those things existed to find a way to fight back against them.

SIX

Civil Disobedience Is an Effective Protest Tactic

Kumi Naidoo

> Kumi Naidoo is the executive director of environmental activist organization Greenpeace. In the following viewpoint he notes that it can seem like governments and corporations are too powerful to oppose and always succeed in furthering their agendas; however, he argues, around the world, activists are succeeding at getting their messages to the public through daring acts of civil disobedience. The author supports his claim by describing several examples of successful protest operations by Greenpeace, such as an incident in which activists boarded a cargo vessel loaded with endangered whale meat, and embarrassed the company into canceling the shipment by climbing the mast and displaying a banner reading "Stop trading in whale meat." Naidoo concludes that it is worthwhile to continue struggling to change the world in positive ways because, as he puts it, "every act of rebellion—no matter how seemingly insignificant—adds up."

Does it all seem too hard? Does it feel like governments and corporations will always get away with it in the end? Do you ask yourself what one person alone can do? Greenpeace is part of a global movement of interconnected people all standing up and joining forces to stop injustices of all kinds. And every day somewhere in the world we're winning.

Earlier today [July 11, 2013], a group of six Greenpeace women activists started climbing western Europe's tallest building, the Shard, in London. As I write, they are still climbing. Their courage and determination is backed by millions of people who have

On June 11, 2013, six women from Greenpeace climbed the Shard building in London to protest oil drilling in the Arctic.

joined the Save the Arctic movement and are asking Shell and others to keep their hands off the Arctic.

They chose to climb the Shard because it towers over Shell's three London offices, including the oil giant's global headquarters on the south bank of the Thames [river]. When they get to the top they plan to hang a piece of Arctic artwork. If they make it, it will be the highest successful art installation since Philippe Petit tightrope-walked between the twin towers of the World Trade Centre [in New York City] in 1974. [The London climbers did reach the top, unfurled a banner reading "Save the Arctic," and were then arrested].

Successful Acts of Civil Disobedience

But this is not all. On Wednesday morning [July 10, 2013] German Greenpeace activists boarded a ship docked in Hamburg [Germany], and prevented it from leaving with a cargo of meat from endangered fin whales hunted off Iceland. Like almost every country in the world, the German government agrees that commercial whaling should be banned. But the authorities decided to let the shipment go. So four activists climbed on to the ship's mooring lines and at the stern of the ship unfurled a banner which said: "Stop trading in whale meat". Suddenly this was looking like more trouble than the cargo company, Charter Unifeeder, wanted. The shipment was cancelled, the meat was not loaded, the activists came off the mooring lines and the ship will leave port short of six containers of whale meat.

And just a couple of days ago [July 9, 2013], Greenpeace activists set up a hanging "nuclear emergency camp" on the suspension cables of the iconic Gwangandaegyo bridge in Busan, South Korea, calling for the government to widen the official nuclear evacuation zone to a 30km [48-mile] radius. The four activists from Korea, USA, Taiwan and Indonesia displayed banners warning the people of Busan that many of them live within that radius. Today, after three days out in the scorching sun and with a great deal of local support from passers by, our team climbed down the cables to attend a meeting at the city hall in Busan.

Relationship Between Environmental Protest and US Environmental Law

According to a study by sociologist Jon Agnon published in 2007, protest is significantly more effective than public opinion in passing pro-environmental federal laws. Agnon claims that every protest event increases the probability of laws that protect the environment being passed by 1.2 percent, and that moderate levels of protest increase the rate at which pro-environmental laws are adopted by 9.5 percent.

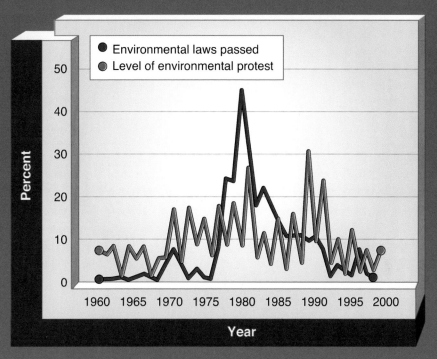

Taken from: Ken Ward. "Convincing Evidence for the Central Role of Protest and a Troubling Cost-Benefit Analysis." Grist, June 20, 2007. http://grist.org/article/where-does-our-power-originate.

The French government agents who bombed the *Rainbow Warrior* [Greenpeace's ship] in Auckland [New Zealand] harbour 28 years ago [1985], thought that their act would silence the anti-nuclear protests in the Pacific. Nothing could have been further from the truth. Many say that activism changed that day. The bombing of the *Rainbow Warrior* was an instance when a government chose to respond to peaceful protest with deadly force, but peaceful protest has prevailed. Peaceful protest has stopped the whale meat transport in Hamburg and catalysed our campaigners meeting with Korean authorities to discuss improved nuclear emergency plans.

It is my hope that our peaceful protest in London today will draw attention to Shell's reckless Arctic drilling plans. The movement to save the Arctic is growing; millions of people are resisting Shell's ambitions to drill for oil in one of the most pristine and unique environments in the world and fast-track climate change. It is obvious that too many corporations and governments do not listen and put power and profit over people, ignoring what is in the best interest of humanity. It is becoming increasingly difficult to get their attention—but one thing that we know that works is civil disobedience and peaceful protest. Every act of rebellion—no matter how seemingly insignificant—adds up.

SEVEN

Protests Like Occupy Damage the Economy and Accomplish Nothing

Frank Manning

Frank Manning is the campaigns coordinator for the Young Britons' Foundation at The College Conservative, an organization founded to provide young conservative activists across the world an opportunity to communicate their conservative values. In the following viewpoint Manning argues that protests like the Occupy movement that took place in the United States and elsewhere in 2011 accomplish little beyond damaging the economy at a time when it is already weakened from various crises. He cites attempted shutdowns of shipping ports in the Pacific Northwest that year as examples of actions that directly damage the capitalist economy on which the protesters and other members of society rely. The author also claims that Occupy camps were riddled with crime and hypocrisy—for example, in London, infrared imaging of the camps at night showed that 90 percent of the tents were empty.

Yet again, the Occupy movement has attempted to shut down ports around America, further damaging the economy and injuring port companies and their workers. While they did this supposedly to express 'solidarity' with various 'martyrs', the 'leaders' of the movement still deny receiving any endorsement from unions operating within the Northwest port area. As a Britain [sic], I want to ask this question: how much further do Occupiers have to push before Americans stand up and say "enough"?

At a time when the worldwide economy needs all the support it can get, protests like these directly cost the American economy millions and millions of dollars in negative publicity and lost productivity which, in turn, hinders growth in the European economy. Therefore, I'm sufficiently pissed.

History will likely place the Occupy protests as a footnote on the global financial crisis. While the Eurozone [the group of nations in Europe using the euro as their national currency] crumbled and American unemployment soared, a collection of socialists, environmentalists, anti-Semites, radicals, statists [those who believe a strong central government should control the economy] and progressives set up camps around the Western world to ask the government to give them something for nothing.

But the Occupy movement has been a blessing to [US president] Barack Obama and Democrats, allowing them the luxury of deflecting their own mistakes onto bankers and businesses rather than facing up to their own failed policies. But its not just American politicians that may be rethinking their support of the Occupy movement. The left-wing Labour party in the UK [United Kingdom] is also reconsidering their supporting role in the Occupy protests. European politicians used the same tactics to shove their failed policies off onto the banking industry and it is going to come back to bite them.

Crime and Hypocrisy in the Occupy Camps

The simple 'bash the bankers, soak the rich' rhetoric has been given too much airtime by liberal media happy to attack a soft tar-

The author argues that protests like the Occupy movement (shown) that took place in the United States and elsewhere in 2011 accomplished little beyond further damaging the economy at a time when it was already weakened from various crises.

get. But not even the noble cause could maintain the high stature of the movement; it lost serious legitimacy when the world heard of the criminality occurring within the camps. Sexual assaults, robberies, thefts and shocking examples of hypocrisy ended any justification for the occupations. Civility was lost and positive attention fled the scene.

Mixed Views of Occupy Wall Street

Despite the populist message of the Occupy Wall Street protests in 2011, public reaction was mixed. According to a Pew Research Center poll in October 2011, support and opposition to the movement was about evenly divided.

Support or oppose movement?	Occupy Wall Street
Support	**39%**
Strongly	16%
Somewhat	23%
Oppose	**35%**
Strongly	16%
Somewhat	19%
Neither	**6%**
Do Not Know	**20%**

Taken from: "Public Divided Over Occupy Wall Street Movement." Pew Research Center for the People & the Press, October 24, 2011. www.people-press.org/2011/10/24/public-divided-over-occupy-wall-street-movement/?src=prc-headline.

In the Occupy London protest, police used a thermal imaging camera to examine the tents. The majority of the them, almost 90%, were empty at night. These rent-a-cause protestors were hanging around the camp in the daytime then going home to their warm, capitalist beds in the evening. Hardly 'solidarity' at its finest.

The icy chill of winter will inevitably send the majority of protestors home, and it is likely that the entire Occupy 'movement' will end in a damp squib [a firecracker that fizzles out instead of bursts] rather than a final conflict. The cost of policing and cleaning all of their camps will run into millions of dollars though, a cost which will be generously met by, you guessed it, the taxpayers of America.

Without realizing it, the Occupy movement has been used by everyone. To the media, they are a quick story they can stretch out for months. To Republicans, they are an example of modern-day entitlement culture, young people who expect the moon on a stick and refuse to work for it. To Democrats, they are useful idiots, taking media attention off Obama's diabolical ratings.

EIGHT

The Occupy Movement Had a Lasting Impact

Rebecca Solnit

San Francisco, California, writer Rebecca Solnit is the author of *Hope in the Dark: Untold Histories, Wild Possibilities*. During the height of the Occupy protest movement in 2011 she participated in Occupy Wall Street, Occupy San Francisco, and Occupy Oakland. In the following viewpoint she argues that the Occupy movement changed the national conversation, focusing attention on how the wealthiest 1 percent of the population wields a disproportionate amount of political and economic power in the United States, to the disadvantage of the remaining 99 percent of the population. She claims that the severity and brutality of the police crackdown on the movement showed how afraid the wealthy are of such ideas gaining traction in society. Perhaps the greatest impact of the Occupy movement, she suggests, was the effect it had on those who took part in it, showing them what is possible and how much potential power they have to effect change.

I would have liked to know what the drummer hoped and what she expected. We'll never know why she decided to take a drum to the central markets of Paris [France] on October 5, 1789, and why, that day, the tinder was so ready to catch fire and a drumbeat was one of the sparks.

To the beat of that drum, the working women of the market-place marched all the way to the Palace of Versailles, a dozen miles away, occupied the seat of French royal power, forced the king back to Paris, and got the French Revolution rolling. Far more than with the storming of the Bastille almost three months earlier, it was then that the revolution was really launched—though both were mysterious moments when citizens felt impelled to act and acted together, becoming in the process that mystical body, civil society, the colossus who writes history with her feet and crumples governments with her bare hands. . . .

Such transformative moments have happened in many times and many places—sometimes as celebratory revolution, sometimes as terrible calamity, sometimes as both, and they are sometimes reenacted as festivals and carnivals. In these moments, the old order is shattered, governments and elites tremble, and in that rupture civil society is born—or reborn.

In the new space that appears, however briefly, the old rules no longer apply. New rules may be written or a counterrevolution may be launched to take back the city or the society, but the moment that counts, the moment never to forget, is the one where civil society is its own rule, taking care of the needy, discussing what is necessary and desirable, improvising the terms of an ideal society for a day, a month, the 10-week duration of the Paris Commune of 1871, or the several weeks' encampment and several-month aftermath of Occupy Oakland [in California in 2011], proudly proclaimed on banners as the Oakland Commune.

Weighing the Meaning of the Occupy Movement

Those who doubt that these moments matter should note how terrified the authorities and elites are when they erupt. That fear is a sign of their recognition that real power doesn't only lie with them. (Sometimes your enemies know what your friends can't believe.) That's why the New York Police Department maintained a massive presence at Occupy Wall Street's [OWS's] encampment and spent millions of dollars on punishing the participants (and hundreds of thousands, maybe millions more, in police brutality payouts for all the clubbing and pepper-gassing of unarmed ideal-ists, as well as $47,000 for the destruction of the OWS library, because in situations like these a library is a threat, too).

Those who dismiss these moments because of their flaws need to look harder at what joy and hope shine out of them and what real changes have, historically, emerged because of them, even if not always directly or in the most obvious or recognizable ways. Change is rarely as simple as dominos. Sometimes, it's as complex as chaos theory and as slow as evolution. Even things that seem to happen suddenly turn out to be flowers that emerge from plants with deep roots in the past or sometimes from long-dormant seeds.

It's important to ask not only what those moments produced in the long run but what they were in their heyday. If people find themselves living in a world in which some hopes are realized, some joys are incandescent, and some boundaries between indi-viduals and groups are lowered, even for an hour or a day or—in the case of Occupy Wall Street—several months, that matters.

The old left imagined that victory would, when it came, be total and permanent, which is practically the same as saying that victory was and is impossible and will never come. It is, in fact, more than possible. It is something that participants have tasted many times and that we carry with us in many ways, however flawed and fleeting. We regularly taste failure, too. Most of the time, the two come mixed and mingled. And every now and then, the possibilities explode.

In these moments of rupture, people find themselves members of a "we" that did not until then exist. . . . New possibilities suddenly emerge, or that old dream of a just society reemerges and—at least for a little while—shines. . . .

I have often heard that Freedom Summer in Mississippi reg-istered some [previously excluded African American] voters and built some alliances in 1964, but that its lasting (if almost impossi-ble to measure) impact, was on the young participants themselves. They were galvanized into a feeling of power, of commitment, of mission that seems to have changed many of them and stayed with them as they went on to do a thousand different things that

During the Occupy Wall Street protests, the New York Police Department maintained a massive presence at Occupy Wall Street's encampment and spent millions of dollars on arresting and punishing the participants.

mattered, as they helped build the antiauthoritarian revolution that has been slowly unfolding, here and elsewhere, over the last half century or so. By such standards, when it comes to judging the effects of Occupy, it's far too soon to tell—and as with so many moments and movements, we may never fully know. . . .

Changing the National Conversation

Almost as soon as Occupy Wall Street appeared in the fall of 2011, it was clear that the national conversation had changed, that the brutality and obscenity of Wall Street was suddenly being openly discussed, that the suffering of ordinary people crushed by the burden of medical, housing, or college debt was coming out of the shadows, that the Occupy encampments had become places where people could testify about the destruction of their hopes and lives. California passed a homeowner's bill of rights to curtail the viciousness of the banks, and in late 2012 Strike Debt emerged as an Occupy offshoot to address indebtedness in creative and subversive ways. Student debt suddenly became (and remains) a topic of national discussion, and proposals for student loan reform began to gain traction. Invisible suffering had been made visible.

Change often happens by making the brutality of the status quo visible and so intolerable. The situation everybody has been living in is suddenly described in a new way by a previously silenced or impacted constituency, or with new eloquence, or because our ideas of what is humane and decent evolve, or a combination of all three. Thus did slavery become intolerable to ever more free people before the Civil War. Thus did the rights of many groups in this country—women, people of color, queer people, disabled people—grow exponentially. Thus did marriage stop being an exclusive privilege of heterosexuality, and earlier, a hierarchical relationship between a dominant husband and a submissive wife.

When the Silent Speak

Occupy Wall Street allowed those silenced by shame, invisibility, or lack of interest from the media to speak up. As a result, the realities behind our particular economic game came to be described more accurately; so much so that the media and politicians had to change their language a little to adjust to—admit to—a series of previously ignored ugly realities. This, in turn, had consequences, even if they weren't always measurable or sometimes even immediately detectable.

Though Occupy was never primarily about electoral politics, it was nonetheless a significant part of the conversation that got Elizabeth Warren elected [US] senator [from Massachusetts] and a few other politicians doing good things in the cesspit of the capital. As Occupy was, in part, sparked by the vision of the Arab Spring [widespread antigovernment protests in the Middle East], so its mood of upheaval and outrage might have helped spark Idle No More, the dynamic Native peoples' movement [2012 onward]. Idle No More has already become a vital part of the environmental and climate movements and, in turn, has sparked a resurgence of Native American and Native Canadian activism.

Occupy Wall Street also built alliances around racist persecution that lasted well after most of the encampments were disbanded. Occupiers were there for everything from the Million Hoodie Marches to protest the slaying of Trayvon Martin [young unarmed African American pedestrian fatally shot by white man later acquitted of the crime] in Florida to stop-and-frisk in New York City to racist bank policies and foreclosures in San Francisco. There, a broad-based housing rights movement came out of Occupy that joined forces with the Alliance of Californians for Community Empowerment (ACCE) to address foreclosures, evictions, corrupt banking practices, and more. Last week [in early September 2012] a conservative warned that "Occupy may soon occupy New York's City Hall," decrying mayoral front-runner [who was eventually elected] Bill de Blasio's economic populism, alleged support for Occupy, and opposition to stop-and-frisk. . . .

Highlighting Economic Inequality

Part of what gave Occupy its particular beauty was the way the movement defined "we" as the 99% [everyone not included in the top 1 percent of wealthiest Americans]. That (and that contagious meme the 1%) entered our language, offering a way of imagining the world [as] so much more inclusive than just about anything that had preceded it. And what an inclusive movement it was: the usual young white suspects, from really privileged to really desperate, but also a range of participants from World War II to Iraq War veterans to former Black Panthers [African American activists], from libertarians to liberals to anarchist insurrectionists, from the tenured to the homeless to hip-hop moguls and rock stars.

And there was so much brutality, too, from the young women pepper-sprayed at an early Occupy demonstration and the students infamously pepper-sprayed while sitting peacefully on the

Public Perceptions of Conflict Between Rich and Poor, 2009 and 2011

The Occupy Wall Street protests in 2011 had a significant impact on public opinion, highlighting the issue of extreme wealth inequality in the United States and significantly increasing the perception of class conflict between the rich and the poor.

Percent who say there are "very strong" or "strong" conflicts between the rich and the poor.

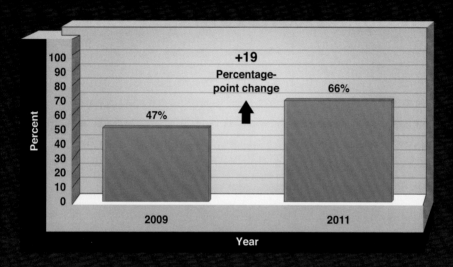

Taken from: Rich Morin. "Rising Share of Americans See Conflict Between Rich and Poor." Pew Research Social & Demographic Trends, January 11, 2012. www.pewsocialtrends.org/2012/01/11/rising-share-of-americans-see -conflict-between-rich-and-poor/.

campus of the University of California, Davis, to the poet laureate Robert Hass clubbed in the ribs at the Berkeley encampment, 84-year-old Dorli Rainey assaulted by police at Occupy Seattle, and the Iraq War veteran Scott Olsen whose skull was fractured by a projectile fired by the Oakland police. And then, of course, there was the massive police presence and violent way that in a number of cities the movement's occupiers were finally ejected from their places of "occupation."

Such overwhelming institutional violence couldn't have made clearer the degree to which the 1% considered Occupy a genuine threat. At the G-20 economic summit [a meeting of the top twenty world economies] in 2011, the Russian Prime Minister, Dmitry Medvedev, said, "The reward system of shareholders and managers of financial institution[s] should be changed step by step. Otherwise the 'Occupy Wall Street' slogan will become fashionable in all developed countries." That was the voice of fear, because the realized dreams of the 99% are guaranteed to be the 1%'s nightmares. . . .

Occupy encampments and general assemblies spread from Auckland [New Zealand] to Hong Kong [China], from Oakland [California] to London [England] in the fall of 2011. Some of them lasted well into 2012, and others spawned things that are still with us: coalitions and alliances and senses of possibility and frameworks for understanding what's wrong and what could be right. It was a sea-change moment, a watershed movement, a dream realized imperfectly (because only unrealized dreams are perfect), a groundswell that remains ground on which to build.

On the second anniversary of that day [September 17, 2011] in lower Manhattan when people first sat down in outrage and then stayed in dedication and solidarity and hope, remember them, remember how unpredictably the world changes, remember those doing heroic work that you might hear little or nothing about but who are all around you, remember to hope, remember to build. Remember that you are 99% likely to be one of them and take up the burden that is also an invitation to change the world and occupy your dreams.

NINE

Economic Inequality in the United States Is an Important Issue for Protest Movements

Leif Dautch

> Leif Dautch is a deputy attorney general at the California Department of Justice. In the following viewpoint Dautch argues that the 2011 Occupy protests were motivated by a belief that the very wealthy have a moral responsibility to help those in society struggling to make ends meet, and that the ultrarich are not meeting that responsibility. Any plan—such as President Barack Obama's 2011 jobs bill—that would increase taxes on the wealthiest 1 percent of Americans to help out the poorest of the rest of the 99 percent of society generates significant political opposition. According to Dautch, the ultrarich have in the past paid a much higher percentage of income tax than they do now (e.g., 70 percent in 1980 versus 35 percent in 2011). As long as the very rich continue to shirk their moral duty to contribute fairly to rebuild a healthy economy, Dautch contends, economic inequality will continue to be a legitimate and powerful motivation for protest.

Critics of the "Occupy Wall Street" movement note that protesters lack a fine-tuned political or economic message. But this critique misses the point. The unifying principle of the movement is not based on political or economic theory, but instead on a quintessentially moral theme.

The signs say it best. From "Robin Hood Was Right" to "Hey You Billionaires: Pay Your Fair Share," the movement's core

The author claims the unifying principle of the Occupy movement is not based on political or economic theory but instead on a quintessentially moral theme of economic equality.

principle is an appeal to fundamental fairness and the belief that the highest-earning among us should help those struggling to meet the basic needs of life. Although religion has no monopoly on social morality, one might recognize the concept as a core tenet of, among other religions, Christianity: the claimed faith of 80% of Tea Party members and 95% of GOP [Grand Old Party, i.e., the Republican Party] members of Congress.

The outrage that spawned Occupy has many causes, from staggeringly high unemployment rates to proposed cuts to government services. But thousands of people didn't march on [New York's] Times Square in 1982 when the nationwide unemployment rate neared 11%. And town squares across the country haven't filled with protesters every time politicians preached fiscal austerity.

Rejection by Ultrarich

Instead, the catalyst for the Occupy movement was the perceived rejection by the ultrarich—or at least by the politicians who represent the ultrarich—of this notion of social morality. If the debt-ceiling crisis and the defeat of President [Barack] Obama's jobs bill revealed anything, it was the reluctance of the top 1% to shoulder any significant burden in the country's efforts to rebuild the economy and put people back to work. It was these public displays of indifference that ignited the discontent of the 99%.

In a way, the protesters' decision to frame their demands in moral terms is good strategy. Economics is premised on the assumption that people will act solely in their best interest. Morality is one of the few remaining realms in which individuals are occasionally expected to act for another's benefit.

Protests' Honest Approach

The movement's decision to frame the debate in moral terms is also refreshingly honest. The core strength of Occupy lies in the implicit admission that perhaps the top 1% will never derive government benefits equal to the tax bill they are asked to foot. Nonetheless, the movement contends, the ultrarich have a moral responsibility to help rebuild the middle class, to help put people

According to a report by Professor G. William Domhoff of the University of California at Santa Cruz, wealth in the United States is very unevenly distributed, with the richest 1 percent of the population possessing 42 percent of the total financial wealth and the poorest 80 percent of the population collectively owning only 5 percent.

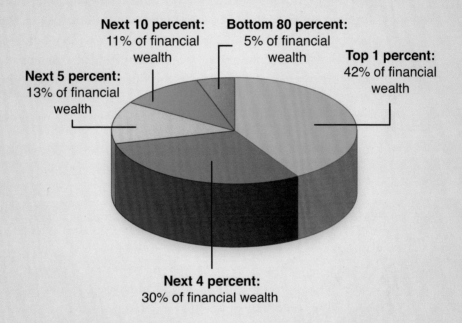

Next 10 percent: 11% of financial wealth

Bottom 80 percent: 5% of financial wealth

Top 1 percent: 42% of financial wealth

Next 5 percent: 13% of financial wealth

Next 4 percent: 30% of financial wealth

Taken from: G. William Domhoff. "Wealth, Income, and Power." Who Rules America? February 2013. www2.ucsc.edu/whorulesamerica/power/wealth.html.

back to work, to help shore up the health of our economy. And let's be honest: Each of the proposed fixes for the employment crisis—from lowering payroll taxes to direct government investment in infrastructure projects—will require the government to raise revenue. And revenue means taxes.

"Socialism!" some pundits cry. But asking the ultrarich to contribute to our economic rehabilitation is not socialism. It's the way this country has functioned since ratification of the 16th

Amendment in 1913 gave Congress the authority to establish the modern income tax. In fact, today's top 1% are asked to shoulder a far lighter tax burden than their wealthy forebears. Today's [2011] top federal income tax bracket is 35%; in 1918 it was 77%. In 1952 it was 92%. As recently as 1980, it was 70%.

The protesters will not relent until the ultrarich embrace this norm of social morality. How that transformation will manifest is unclear, but a symbolic first step would be passage of a "millionaire's tax" akin to that proposed by Senate Democrats in Obama's jobs bill. Such a measure would not only provide much-needed revenue for the economic recovery, but would also reflect at least partial recognition of the ultrarich's duty to help those in need.

TEN

Protest Movements Targeting Economic Inequality in the United States Are Misguided

Investor's Business Daily

The following selection is taken from an editorial by *Investor's Business Daily*, a national US newspaper serving the financial investment community. The author argues that recent protest movements in the United States against income inequality are based on misunderstandings. The first is that people are stuck in particular income brackets; i.e., if they are born poor they will remain poor. The author claims that income mobility—movement of people in and out of economic classes—is high in America; someone protesting against the richest 1 percent of society today may be a member of the 1 percent later in life. Secondly, the author refutes claims that the rich do not pay their fair share of taxes, as is commonly believed, pointing out that the top 1 percent pay 40 percent of total income tax revenue. Finally, the author says that the poor benefit from generous subsidies largely paid for by taxes paid by the wealthy.

Inequality: President [Barack] Obama's class-envy strategy is built on a false premise—that the rich get richer at the expense of the poor. Amazingly, such zero-sum thinking is influencing public opinion.

Twice as many Americans support the anti–Wall Street protesters as oppose them. And even Rasmussen is polling [in 2011] that nearly half of Americans support proposals to soak the rich.

This is an emotional response to both the hard economic times and dishonest political rhetoric. People are buying into the notion peddled by the left that the rich steal from people. It's a pernicious myth left over from preindustrial Marxism.

The left says current levels of income inequality echo the late 1920s and the Gilded Age [1870s–1900]. They've zeroed in on the richest 1%, citing Census Bureau data showing these top earners "grabbing" more income than the bottom 90%.

But the census stats are misleading.

Income Mobility

For one, they are a snapshot of income distribution at a single point in time. Yet income is not static. It changes over time. Low-paying jobs from early adulthood give way to better-paying jobs later in life.

And income groups in America are not fixed. There's no caste system here, really no such thing even as a middle "class." The poor aren't stuck in poverty. And the rich don't enjoy lifetime membership in an exclusive club.

A 2007 Treasury Department study bears this out. Nearly 58% of U.S. households in the lowest-income quintile [one-fifth of the population] in 1996 moved to a higher level by 2005. The reverse also held true. Of those households that were in the top 1% in income in 1996, more than 57% dropped to a lower-income group by 2005.

Every day in America, the poor join the ranks of the rich, and the rich fall out of comfort.

So even if income equality is increasing, it does not mean income mobility is decreasing. There is still a great deal of movement in and out of the richest and poorest groups in America.

Percent of Individuals in the United States with Family Income Above Their Parents, by Parents' Income Level, 2012

According to a report from the Pew Charitable Trusts Economic Mobility Project, the majority of adults in the United States have a higher income than that of their parents. Ninety-three percent of people raised in the bottom quintile (i.e., the poorest one-fifth of the population) had an income level higher than that of their parents.

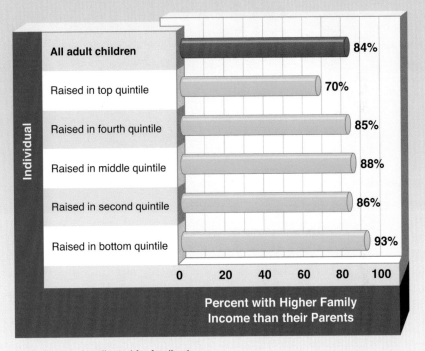

Individual	Percent with Higher Family Income than their Parents
All adult children	84%
Raised in top quintile	70%
Raised in fourth quintile	85%
Raised in middle quintile	88%
Raised in second quintile	86%
Raised in bottom quintile	93%

Note: Income is adjusted for family size.

Taken from: "Pursuing the American Dream: Economic Mobility Across Generations." The Pew Charitable Trusts Economic Mobility Project, July 2012. www.pewstates.org/uploadedFiles/PCS_Assets/2012/Pursuing_American_Dream.pdf.

A Bounty of Subsidies for the Poor

The beauty of our free-market system (what's left of it), is that even among the thousands of Wall Street protesters thumping, "We are the 99%," there are those who might not be able to say that a decade or so from now. Some might go on to profit from

Those that disagree with Occupy's stand on income equality assert that the rich do not fail to pay their fair share of taxes, as is commonly believed, pointing out that the wealthiest 1 percent of the nation pays 40 percent of total income tax revenue.

an Internet start-up. Others might get a rap contract. Anything's possible in America.

One of those street agitators might even become president, following in the shoes of Obama, who's now one of the 1-percenters he mocks.

Another problem with the census data is they don't include the noncash income received by the lowest-income households. Each year, the poor get tens of billions of dollars in subsidies for housing, food and health care. None of these transfer payments, a lot of it paid for by the 1%, is counted as income by the Census Bureau.

One report estimates that the share of total income earned by the lowest-income group would rise roughly 50% if such welfare were considered.

Most Income Tax Is Paid by the Very Rich

Likewise, the share of total income earned by the top income quintile would drop about 7% if taxes paid to fund welfare were considered.

Census doesn't take into account the equalizing effects of taxes. Though they earn more than 45% of total income, the top 10% of taxpayers pay over 70% of the total income-tax burden. The top 1%? They shoulder a whopping 40% of the tax load.

Federal Reserve and other data—which include all financial and nonfinancial assets, including bank accounts, investments, houses and cars—give a more complete picture of the gap. When you count all wealth, not just income, inequality has not gotten worse.

The top 1% account for 35% of total wealth [in 2011], compared with 37% in 1922. In fact, the worst wealth disparity ever was in the 1990s under [Democratic] President [Bill] Clinton.

ELEVEN

From Slacktivism to Activism

Evgeny Morozov

> Evgeny Morozov is a contributing editor at the *New Republic* and is the author of *To Save Everything, Click Here: The Folly of Technological Solutionism*. In the following viewpoint Morozov asserts that use of social media such as Facebook by activists typically leads to what he calls "slacktivism," in which trivial online activities replace meaningful action in the real world. Someone may join a Facebook page supporting a particular cause or forward information to their online acquaintances and believe they have made a contribution and are finished; however, they have not actually done anything that substantially furthers the cause, he maintains. Morozov recommends that protest organizations change their approach to take into account the potentials and pitfalls of how things work online; for example, instead of trying to attract large numbers of people, they could narrow their focus and look for fewer people who are willing to do more work.

As someone who studies how the Internet affects global politics, I've grown increasingly skeptical of numerous digital activism campaigns that attempt to change the world through Facebook and Twitter. To explain why, let me first tell you a story about a campaign that has gone wrong.

If you have been to Copenhagen, you probably have seen the Stork Fountain, the city's famous landmark. A few months ago, Danish psychologist Anders Colding-Jørgensen, who studies how ideas spread online, used Facebook to conduct a little experiment using the Stork Fountain as his main subject. He started a Facebook group, which implied—but never stated so explicitly— that the city authorities were planning to dismantle the fountain, which of course was NEVER the case. He seeded the group to 125 friends who joined in a matter of hours; then it started spreading virally. In the first few days, it immediately went to 1000 members and then it started growing more aggressively. After 3 days, it began to grow with over 2 new members each minute in the day time. When the group reached 27,500 members, Jørgensen decided to end the experiment. So there you have it: almost 28,000 people joined a cause that didn't really exist! As far as "clouds" go, that one was probably an empty one.

This broaches an interesting question: why do people join Facebook groups in the first place? In an interview with the *Washington Post*, Jørgensen said that "just like we need stuff to furnish our homes to show who we are, on Facebook we need cultural objects that put together a version of me that I would like to present to the public." Other researchers agree: studies by Sherri Grasmuck, a sociologist at Temple University, reveals that Facebook users shape their online identity implicitly rather than explicitly: that is, the kind of campaigns and groups they join reveals more about who they are than their dull "about me" page.

This shopping binge in an online identity supermarket has led to the proliferation of what I call "slacktivism," where our digital efforts make us feel very useful and important but have zero social impact. When the marginal cost of joining yet another Facebook group are low, we click "yes" without even blinking, but the truth is that it may distract us from helping the same cause in more productive ways. Paradoxically, it often means that the very act of joining a Facebook group is often the end—rather than the beginning—of our engagement with a cause, which undermines much of digital activism.

According to data from the Digitial Activism Research Project at the University of Washington, the number of cases in which activists used digital technology in social protests to effect social or political change from 1990 to 2009 increased dramatically starting in 2006. Critics of online activism contend that despite such increased use, digital tools are of minimal or secondary importance in achieving the goals of social protest movements.

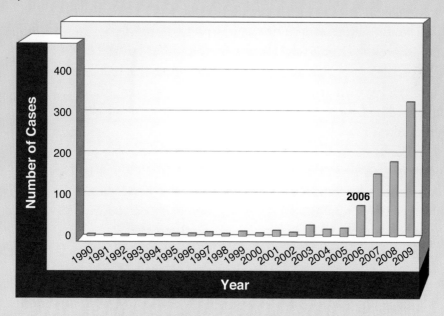

Taken from: Mary C. Joyce. "The Proof Is in the Pendulum: A History of Digital Activism and Repression." OWNI, September 23, 2011. http:owni.eu/2011/09/23/the-proof-is-in-the-pendulum-a-history-of-digital-activism-and -repression/.

Take a popular Facebook group "saving the children of Africa." It looks very impressive—over 1.2 million members—until you discover that these compassionate souls have raised about $6,000 (or half a penny per person). In a perfect world, this shouldn't even be considered a problem: better donate a penny than not to donate at all. The problem, however, is that the granularity of contemporary digital activism provides too many easy way-

outs: too many people decide to donate a penny where they may otherwise want to donate a dollar.

So, what exactly plagues most "slacktivist" campaigns? Above all, it's their unrealistic assumption that, given enough awareness, all problems are solvable; or, in the language of computer geeks, given enough eyeballs all bugs are shallow. This is precisely what propels many of these campaigns into gathering signatures, adding new members to their Facebook pages, and asking everyone involved to link to the campaign on blogs and Twitter. This works for some issues—especially local ones. But global bugs—like climate change—are bugs of a different nature. Thus, for most global problems, whether it's genocide in Darfur or climate change, there are diminishing returns to awareness-raising. At some point one simply needs to learn how to convert awareness into action—and this is where tools like Twitter and Facebook prove much less useful.

This is not to deny that many of the latest digital activism initiatives, following the success of the Obama electoral juggernaut, have managed to convert their gigantic membership lists into successful money-raising operations. The advent of micro-donations—whereby one can donate any sum from a few cents to a few dollars—has enabled [organizations] to raise funds that could then be used—at least, in theory—to further advance the goals of the campaign. The problem is that most of these campaigns do not have clear goals or agenda items beyond awareness-raising.

Besides, not every problem can be solved with an injection of funds, which, in a way, creates the same problem as awareness-raising: whether it's financial capital or media capital, spending it in a way that would enable social change could be very tough. Asking for money could also undermine one's efforts to engage group members in more meaningful real-life activities: the fact that they have already donated some money, no matter how little, makes them feel as if they have already done their bit and should be left alone.

Some grassroots campaigns are beginning to realize it: for example, the web-site of "Free Monem," a 2007 pan-Arab initiative to free an Egyptian blogger from jail carried a sign that said "DON'T

DONATE; Take action" and had logos of Visa and MasterCard in a crossed red circle in the background. According to Sami Ben Gharbia, a Tunisian Internet activist and one of the organizers of the campaign, this was a way to show that their campaign needed more than money as well as to shame numerous local and international NGOs that like to raise money to "release bloggers from jail," without having any meaningful impact on the situation on the ground.

That said, the meager fund-raising results of the Save the Children of Africa campaign still look quite puzzling. Surely, even a dozen people working together would be able to raise more money. Could it be that the Facebook environment is putting too many restraints on how they might otherwise have decided to cooperate?

Psychologists offer an interesting explanation as to why a million people working together may be less effective than one person working alone. They call this phenomenon "social loafing." It was discovered by the French scientist Max Ringelmann in 1913, when he asked a group of men to pull on a rope. It turned out they each pulled less hard than when they had to pull alone; this was basically the opposite of synergy. Experiments prove that we usually put much less effort into a task when other people are also doing it with us (think about the last time you had to sing a Happy Birthday song). The key lesson here is that when everyone in the group performs the same mundane tasks, it's impossible to evaluate individual contributions; thus, people inevitably begin slacking off. Increasing the number of other persons diminishes the relative social pressure on each person. That's, in short, what Ringelmann called "social loafing."

Reading about Ringelmann's experiments, I realized that the same problem plagues much of today's "Facebook" activism: once we join a group, we move at the group's own pace, even though we could have been much more effective on our own. As you might have heard from Ethan Zuckerman, Facebook and Twitter were not set up for activists by activists; they were set up for the purposes of entertainment and often attracted activists not because they offered unique services but because they were hard to

Belarusian writer Evgeny Morozov (pictured), an expert on the social implications of technology, recommends that protest organizations change their approach to take into account the potentials and pitfalls of how things work online.

block. Thus, we shouldn't take it for granted that Facebook activism is the ultimate limit of what's possible in the digital space; it is just the first layer of what's possible if you work on a budget and do not have much time to plan your campaign.

So far, the most successful "slacktivist" initiatives have been those that have set realistic expectations and have taken advantage of "slacktivist" inclinations of Internet users rather than deny their existence. For example, FreeRice, a web-site affiliated with the UN Food Program, which contains numerous education games, the most popular of which are those helping you to learn English. While you are doing so, it exposes you to online ads, the proceeds of which go towards purchasing and distributing rice in the poor countries (by FreeRice's estimates, enough rice is being distributed to feed 7,000 people daily).

This is a brilliant approach: millions of people rely on the Internet to study English anyway and most of them wouldn't mind being exposed to online advertising in exchange for a useful service. Both sides benefit, with no high words exchanged. Those who participate in the effort are not driven by helping the world and have a very selfish motivation; yet, they probably generate more good than thousands of people who are "fighting" hunger via Facebook. While this model may not be applicable to every situation, it's by finding practical hybrid models like FreeRice's that we could convert immense and undeniable collective energy of Internet users into tangible social change.

So, given all this, how do we avoid "slacktivism" when designing an online campaign? First, make it hard for your supporters to become a slacktivist: don't give people their identity trophies until they have proved their worth. The merit badge should come as a result of their successful and effective contributions to your campaign rather than precede it.

Second, create diverse, distinctive, and non-trivial tasks; your supporters can do more than just click "send to all" button all day. Since most digital activism campaigns are bound to suffer from the problem of diffusion of responsibility, make it impossible for your supporters to fade into the crowd and "free ride" on the work of other people. Don't give up easily: the giant identity supermarket that Facebook has created could actually be a boon for those organizing a campaign; they just need to figure out a way in which to capitalize on identity aspiration of "slacktivists" by giving them interesting and meaningful tasks that could then be evaluated.

Third, do not overdose yourself on the Wikipedia model. It works for some tasks but for most—it doesn't. While inserting a comma into yet another trivia article on Wikipedia does help, being yet another invisible "slacktivist" doesn't. Finding the lowest common denominator between a million users may ultimately yield lower results than raising the barrier and forcing the activists to put up more rather than less effort into what they are doing. Anyone who tells you otherwise is insane. Or, worse, a slacker! Thank you.

TWELVE

Social Media Amplify the Power of Protest

Mathew Ingram

> Mathew Ingram is a senior writer with the journalistic website Gigaom, where he covers media, web culture, and related issues. In the following viewpoint Ingram argues that while social media and related tools may not ultimately cause protest movements to happen, they can greatly facilitate and accelerate the process. Ingram examines the revolutions that happened in Tunisia and Egypt in 2010 and 2011, and acknowledges that there were deep causes of people's discontent in those countries—such as repressive dictatorships and widespread poverty—that preexisted social media and that revolution would have happened without such online tools. He claims, however, that networked communication through services such as Twitter and Facebook powerfully augmented the protests by facilitating connections between people inside the country, getting the word out to people and organizations outside the country who supported the aims of the protesters, and helping the protest groups to organize their efforts.

Just as it was during the recent uprisings in Tunisia [December 2010–January 2011]; the role of social media in the recent upheaval in Egypt has been the subject of much debate since the unrest began on Thursday [January 27, 2011]. *Daily Show* host

Jon Stewart on Friday [January 28, 2011,] poked fun at the idea that Twitter might have played a key part in the demonstrations, and there are many observers who share his skepticism. The real trigger for the uprisings, they argue, is simply the frustration of the oppressed Egyptian people—which is undoubtedly true. But it also

A Tunisian student uses social media to keep up with the protests in her country. Social media can be incredibly powerful tools for spreading the word, giving moral or emotional support to others in a given country, and generating external support, the author claims.

seems clear that social media [have] played a key role in getting the word out, and in helping organizers plan their protests. In the end, it's not about Twitter or Facebook: it's about the power of real-time networked communication.

Social Media Are Effective Tools for Protesters

Foreign Policy magazine columnist Evgeny Morozov has argued that Twitter and Facebook should not be credited with playing any kind of critical role in Tunisia, and suggested that doing so is a sign of the "cyber-utopianism" that many social-media advocates suffer from: that is, the belief that the Internet is unambiguously good, or that the use of Twitter or Facebook can somehow magically free a repressed society from its shackles. Morozov, who has written an entire book about this idea called *Net Delusion*, made the point in his blog post after the Tunisian uprising that while social media might have been used in some way during the events, tools like Twitter and Facebook did not play a crucial role—that is, the revolution would have happened with or without them.

Zeynep Tufekci, a professor of sociology who has also looked at this issue, described in a post following the revolution in Tunisia how professional observers distinguish between what she called "material," "efficient" and "final" causes—in other words, things that are required in order to produce a certain outcome, and things that are nice to have but are not a requirement. Tufekci argues that social media *was* a crucial factor in Tunisia, while Jillian York of Global Voices Online believes that social media tools are useful, but not necessary. Ethan Zuckerman, one of the founders of Global Voices Online, has also written about how the uprisings in both Tunisia and in Egypt have more to do with decades of poverty and repressive dictatorships than they do with social media.

But is anyone really arguing that Twitter and Facebook *caused* the revolutions in Tunisia or Egypt, or even the earlier public uprisings in Moldova or Iran for that matter? Maybe cyber-utopians somewhere are doing this, but I haven't seen or heard of any. The argument I have tried to make is simply that they and other social media tools can be incredibly powerful, both for spreading the

Political Engagement on Social Networking Sites (SNS), 2013

According to the study "Civic Engagements in the Digital Age," published in April, 2013, 60 percent of American adults participate in social networking sites such as Google+, Twitter, or Facebook. The chart shows what percentage of users participate in various political behaviors.

	Percent of SNS users who have done this	Percent of all adults who have done this
"Like" or promote material related to political/ social issues that others have posted	38%	23%
Encourage other people to vote	35%	21%
Post your own thoughts/comments on political or social issues	34%	20%
Report content related to political/social issues	33%	19%
Encourage others to take action on political/ social issues that are important to you	31%	19%
Post links to political stories or articles for others to read	28%	17%
Belong to a group that is involved in political/ social issues, or working to advance a cause	21%	12%
Follow elected officials, candidates for office, or other public figures	20%	12%
Total who said yes to any of the activities listed above	**66%**	**39%**

Taken from: Aaron Smith. "Civil Engagement in the Digital Age." Pew Internet, April 25, 2013.
www.pewinternet.org/Reports/2013/Civic-Engagement/Summary-of-Findings.aspx.

word—which can give moral or emotional support to others in a country, as well as generating external support—as well as for organizational purposes, thanks to the power of the network. As Jared Cohen of Google Ideas put it, social media may not be a cause, but it can be a powerful "accelerant."

The Growing Power of Networked Communication

Did Twitter or Facebook cause the Tunisian revolt? No. But they did spread the news, and many Tunisian revolutionaries gave them a lot of credit for helping with the process. Did Twitter cause the revolts in Egypt? No. But they did help activists such as WikiLeaks supporter Jacob Appelbaum (known on Twitter as @ioerror) and others as they organized the dialup and satellite phone connections that created an ad-hoc Internet after Egypt turned the real one off—which, of course, it did in large part to try and prevent demonstrators from using Internet-based tools to foment unrest. As [blogger] Cory Doctorow noted in his review of Evgeny Morozov's book, even if Twitter and Facebook are just used to replace the process of stapling pieces of paper to telephone poles and sending out hundreds of emails, they are still a huge benefit to social activism of all kinds.

But open-network advocate Dave Winer made the key point: it's the Internet that is the really powerful tool here, not any of the specific services such as Twitter and Facebook that run on top of it, which Winer compares to brands like NBC. They have power because lots of people use them, and—in the case of Twitter—because they have open protocols so that apps can still access the network even when the company's website is taken down by repressive governments (although they didn't mention Egypt or Tunisia by name, Twitter co-founder Biz Stone and general counsel Alexander Macgillivray wrote a post about the company's desire to "keep the information flowing").

In the end the real weapon is the power of networked communication itself. In previous revolutions it was the fax, or the pamphlet, or the cellphone—now it is SMS [short message service, aka texting] and Twitter and Facebook. Obviously none of these things cause revolutions, but to ignore or downplay their growing importance is also a mistake.

THIRTEEN

This Independence Day, Thank a Protester

Amy Goodman

Amy Goodman is the cofounder, executive producer, and host of the national, daily, independent, award-winning news program *Democracy Now!* and the coauthor of *Standing Up to the Madness: Ordinary Heroes in Extraordinary Times*. In the following viewpoint Goodman argues that protest movements have played a central role in many of the positive changes that have taken place in US society since it was founded, such as the abolitionist movement that freed the slaves, the suffrage movement that won women the right to vote, and the civil rights movement that ended racial segregation. The author points out that vigorous protest movements continue to have beneficial effects, citing as an example the current rights being won by the gay and lesbian community in many states as well as in the military in recent years.

More than 160 years ago, the greatest abolitionist in U.S. history, the escaped slave Frederick Douglass, addressed the Rochester Ladies' Anti-Slavery Society. Douglass asked those gathered, "What, to the American slave, is your Fourth of July?" His words bear repeating this Independence Day, as the United States asserts unprecedented authority to wage war globally, to spy

Edward Snowden (pictured) revealed a vast, global surveillance network implemented by the United States that has outraged citizens and governments the world over.

on everyone, everywhere. Independence Day should serve not as a blind celebration of the government, but as a moment to reflect on the central place in our history of grass-roots democracy movements, which have preserved and expanded the rights proclaimed in the opening lines of the Declaration of Independence: Life, liberty, and the pursuit of happiness.

Douglass answered his question about the Fourth of July to those gathered abolitionists: "To him, your celebration is a sham; your boasted liberty, an unholy license; your national greatness, swelling vanity; your sounds of rejoicing are empty and heartless; your denunciations of tyrants, brass fronted impudence; your shouts of liberty and equality, hollow mockery; your prayers and hymns, your sermons and thanksgivings, with all your religious parade, and solemnity, are, to him, mere bombast, fraud, deception, impiety, and hypocrisy—a thin veil to cover up crimes which would disgrace a nation of savages. There is not a nation on the earth guilty of practices more shocking and bloody, than are the people of these United States, at this very hour."

Douglass not only denounced the hypocrisy of slavery in a democracy, but worked diligently to build the abolitionist movement. He fought for women's suffrage as well. These were movements that have shaped the United States. The civil-rights movement of the 1950s and '60s set a permanent example of what can be achieved by grass-roots action, even in the face of systemic, violent repression.

Today, movements continue to shape our society. The trial of George Zimmerman, accused of murdering Trayvon Martin, would not be happening now in Florida were it not for a mass movement. Sparked by the seeming official indifference to the shooting death of yet another young, African-American male, nationwide protests erupted, leading to the appointment of a special prosecutor. A month and a half after Martin was killed, Zimmerman was charged with second-degree murder.

Gay men and lesbians have seen sweeping changes in their legal rights, as same-sex marriage becomes legal in state after state, the U.S. military has dropped its official discrimination against homosexuality, and the federal Defense of Marriage Act was recently judged unconstitutional. Again, undergirding this progress are the decades of movement-building and grass-roots organizing.

In Egypt, the revolution dubbed The Arab Spring continues, with mass protests forcing out Preident Mohamed Morsi. Where this goes now, with the military in power, is yet to be determined. As my "Democracy Now!" colleague, Sharif Abdel Kouddous, tweeted from the streets of Cairo on the night of the military coup, "After two and a half years, Egypt just went back to square one in its post-Mubarek transition."

The United States has been for well over two centuries a beacon for those around the world suffering under tyranny. But the U.S. also has been the prime global opponent of grass-roots democratic

Social Conflicts in Society

A Pew Research Center report published in January 2012 shows that a high percentage of the US public sees strong conflict between various groups in the United States, creating ripe conditions for social protest movements in the twenty-first century.

Percent who say there are "very strong" or "strong" conflicts between . . .

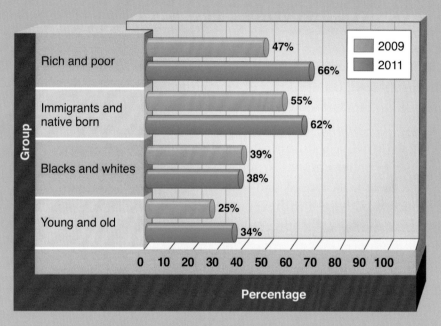

Taken from: Rich Morin. "Rising Share of Americans See Conflict Between Rich and Poor." Pew Research Social & Demographic Trends, January 11, 2012. www.pewsocialtrends.org/2012/11rising-share-of-americans-see-conflict-between-rich-and-poor/.

movements. Amazingly, South African President Nelson Mandela and the African National Congress were not taken off the U.S. terrorist watch list until 2008. When the people of Chile elected Salvador Allende, the U.S. backed a coup against him on Sept. 11, 1973, ushering in the dictatorship of Augusto Pinochet, who murdered thousands of his own citizens, crushing dissent. Sadly, drone strikes and the U.S.-run prison at Guantanamo are not historical references; they are current crimes committed by our own government.

Now, National Security Agency whistle-blower Edward Snowden, as far as we know, is stranded in the Moscow airport, his U.S passport canceled. He has admitted to revealing a vast, global surveillance regime that has outraged citizens and governments the world over. He joins in his plight imprisoned whistle-blower Bradley Manning, who faces life in prison, being court-martialed now for leaking the largest trove of classified documents in U.S. history. WikiLeaks founder Julian Assange has now spent more than a year cooped up in the Ecuadorean Embassy in London. These three are central to the exposure of some of the most undemocratic practices of the U.S. government.

More than 100 protests are planned across the U.S. this July Fourth weekend, in opposition to the NSA's surveillance programs. These protests are part of the continuum of pro-democracy struggles around the world. In closing his Rochester, N.Y., speech, Douglass sounded an optimistic note, saying, "Notwithstanding the dark picture I have this day presented, of the state of the nation, I do not despair of this country." Grass-roots justice movements are the hope, the beacon, the force that will save this country.

FOURTEEN

Popular Dissent Is Being Actively Suppressed in the United States

Chris Hedges

Chris Hedges is a cultural critic and author of *Days of Destruction, Days of Revolt* and *What Every Person Should Know About War*. In 2002 he received the Amnesty International Global Award for Human Rights Journalism. In the following viewpoint Hedges asserts that the government now primarily serves corporate interests regardless of what is good for the people as a whole. According to the author, since protest against the established order is seen as threatening to the corporate state, there are increasing efforts to prevent any protest from taking place. The violent crackdowns on the Occupy protests of 2011 against wealth inequality, as well as arrests of veterans honoring war dead after an official park closing time, are examples of the gradually increasing repression of popular protests. Hedges also notes the increasing use of surveillance to gain advance knowledge of protests and to take preemptive steps to prevent them from happening.

The security and surveillance state, after crushing the Occupy movement and eradicating its encampments, has mounted a relentless and largely clandestine campaign to deny public space to any group or movement that might spawn another popular uprising. The legal system has been grotesquely deformed in most cities to, in essence, shut public space to protesters, eradicating our right to free speech and peaceful assembly.

The goal of the corporate state is to criminalize democratic, popular dissent before there is another popular eruption. The vast state surveillance system, detailed in [former National Security Agency employee] Edward Snowden's revelations to the British newspaper *The Guardian*, at the same time ensures that no action or protest can occur without the advance knowledge of our internal security apparatus. This foreknowledge has allowed the internal security systems to proactively block activists from public spaces as well as carry out pre-emptive harassment, interrogation, intimidation, detention and arrests before protests can begin. There is a word for this type of political system—tyranny.

The Right to Protest Peacefully

If the state is ultimately successful in preventing us from mobilizing in public spaces, then dissent will mutate from nonviolent mass protests to clandestine and perhaps violent acts of resistance. Some demonstrators have already been branded "domestic terrorists" under the law. The rear-guard effort by a handful of activists to protect our rights to be heard and peaceably assemble is perhaps the most crucial, though unseen, struggle we currently are engaged in with the corporate state. It is a struggle to salvage what is left of our civil society and our right to nonviolent resistance against corporate tyranny. This is why the New York City trial last week [in early July 2013] of members of Veterans for Peace, along with other activists, took on an importance that belied the simple trespassing charges against them.

The activists were arrested Oct. 7, 2012, while they were placing flowers in 11 vases and reading the names of the dead inscribed on the wall in New York's Vietnam Veterans Memorial

Plaza after the official closing time, 10 PM. The defiance of the plaza's official closing time—which appears to be enforced against political activists only—was spawned by a May 1, 2012, protest by Occupy Wall Street activists. The Occupy activists had attempted to hold a meeting in the plaza and been driven out by police. A number of Veterans for Peace activists, most of them veterans of the Vietnam War, formed a line in front of the advancing police that May night and refused to move. They were arrested.

Many of these veterans came back to the plaza on a rainy, windy night in October to protest on the 11th anniversary of the invasion of Afghanistan and again assert their right to carry out nonviolent protests in public spaces. They included Jay Wenk, an 86-year-old combat veteran of World War II who served with General George Patton's Third Army in Europe. When he was arrested Wenk was beating a gong in the downpour as the names of the dead were read. During the October protest 25 people were seized by police for refusing to leave the park after 10 PM. Twelve went to trial last week. Manhattan Criminal Court Judge Robert Mandelbaum on Friday [July 12, 2013,] found the dozen activists guilty. The judge, however, quickly threw out his own verdict, calling the case a "unique circumstance." "Justice," he said, "cries out for a dismissal." His dismissal shuts down the possibility of an appeal.

Favoring Corporate Profit Over People

The legislative system, the judicial system, the whole national security state that's invading all of our privacy are taking away our right to dissent," Dr. Margaret Flowers, one of the defendants, told me on a lunch break during the trial. . . .

> But everything that's happening is happening legally. It's a slippery slope. People will look at this case and they're going to say, "So what? They were in a park. There was a rule. It was closing. The police arrested them. That makes sense to me!" And they don't put it in the bigger context. That's how all of this is happening. It's all being justified. The whole system is being flipped on its head. The judicial

Veterans for Peace activists, most of them veterans of the Vietnam War, were arrested at New York's Vietnam Veterans Memorial Plaza for supporting the Occupy protesters who were driven out of the plaza earlier by police.

and law enforcement system should be protecting our rights. We have the right to dissent. It's in the Bill of Rights. The question is, can we halt that slide for a second, maybe even reverse it a little bit?

The executive, legislative and judicial branches of government have been taken over by corporations and used to protect and promote the criminal activity of Wall Street, the destruction of

Public Opinion on Government Anti-Terror Policies

Polling done between 2004 and 2013 shows that an increasing percentage of the US population believes that government anti-terror policies, particularly in terms of surveillance of the general population, have gone too far in restricting civil liberties. Many activists have raised concerns about the potential for widespread surveillance by the state to stifle legitimate social protest movements.

Government Anti-Terror Policies Have . . .

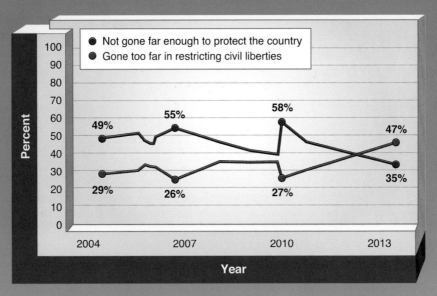

Taken from: "Few See Adequate Limits on NSA Surveillance Program." Pew Research Center for the People & the Press," July 26, 2013. www.people-press.org/2013/07/26/few-see-adequate-limits-on-nsa-surveillance-program/.

the ecosystem by the fossil fuel industry, the looting of the U.S. Treasury by the banking industry and the corporate seizure of all major centers of power. The primacy of corporate profit trumps our right to a living wage, affordable and adequate health care, the regulation of industry and environmental controls, protection from corporate fraud and abuse, the right to a good and affordable public education, the ability to form labor unions, and having a government that serves the basic needs of ordinary citizens. Our voices, our rights and our aspirations are no longer of concern to the state. And if we try to assert them, the state now has mechanisms in place to shut us down.

Defending the Right to Organize in Public Places

Tarak Kauff, a 71-year-old veteran of the Army's 111th Airborne and former professional boxer, was one of the organizers of the Oct. 7 [2012] protest. He has been on a hunger strike for more than a month to express solidarity with the hunger strikers at [the US military prison at] Guantanamo Bay [Cuba] and in the Pelican Bay prison in California. He was gaunt. His skin was ashen and his cheeks sunken. He consumes 300 liquid calories a day and has lost 24 pounds. He was arrested in May [2012] and again in October [2012].

"I saw clearly that the purpose of the arrest was not merely enforcing the 10 PM curfew," he said of the May arrests. . . .

But the purpose was very specific in restricting the right of assembly. We decided that October 7th [2012] would be a perfect day to do it. It was 11 years of war in Afghanistan. So when we came to the Vietnam Veterans Plaza that night we had four purposes. One was to call for an end to the war, the ongoing war in Afghanistan. The second was to call for an end to all U.S. wars of empire. The third was to remember and lament those who had fallen and been wounded in Vietnam, Afghanistan, Iraq, including the civilians, including the 5 million civilians in Vietnam. The fourth was to affirm our right to assemble. If we lose the right to address these issues and to organize in public places, we have absolutely nothing.

"I'm fasting because it's a sacrifice," he said when I asked about his hunger strike. . . . "I want to encourage other people in our movement of the necessity of sacrifice. If we want to establish anything, if we want to re-establish or ever establish any kind of democratic system, it's not going to happen without sacrifice, some kind of sacrifice. And we have a choir. I want to see that choir inspired to start sacrificing more, to take risks. We have to be willing to put our bodies on the line in some way, shape, or form, nonviolently."

Escalating Government Attempts to Stifle Protest

According to several of the activists, some of the police officers said that they too were military veterans and disliked making the arrests but had been told by their superiors to take the demonstrators into custody to prevent another Occupy encampment.

"We can't let you stay," Kauff said he was told by a police captain. "It sets a bad example for the Occupy movement."

"After the process of being arrested began, a police lieutenant told me the Occupy Wall Street people really screwed this up for you guys," Sam Adams, who served in the 101st Airborne Division in Vietnam, said in his courtroom testimony. "You can thank them for this."

The trial was a tiny window into how rattled the state was by Occupy, unfortunately now [as of July 2013] in disarray. The security organs know that as conditions worsen for the majority of Americans, as austerity cuts and chronic unemployment and underemployment drive tens of millions of families into desperation, as climate change continues to produce extreme and dangerous weather, there remains the threat of another popular backlash. The problem lies not, of course, with the Occupy movement, but with the reconfiguration of the government into a handmaiden of corporations that seek to squeeze profits out of the dying carcass of empire.

The corporate state's quest to control all power includes using the military to carry out domestic policing. . . . It is imperative to defend, as the activists did in New York City, what freedoms and rights we have left. If we remain passive, if we permit the state to continue to use the law to take away our right of political expression, we will have no legal protection of resistance when we will need it most.

What You Should Know About Social Protest

Political and Protest Activity Online and Offline

According to a survey by the Pew Internet & American Life Project conducted in August 2013:

- In the year prior to the survey, 48 percent of US adults participated in a civic activity or group; of those who so participated:
    - 35 percent worked with other citizens to solve a community problem;
    - 22 percent went to a political meeting about school, town, or local affairs;
    - 13 percent were actively involved with a group attempting to influence the government or public;
    - 10 percent went to a political speech or rally;
    - 7 percent volunteered or worked for a political candidate or party; and
    - 6 percent went to an organized protest.
- Thirty-nine percent of US adults spoke out in a public forum or communicated with a government official about an issue important to them, using offline means; 34 percent did so using online means.
- Twenty-two percent of US adults signed a paper petition recently; 17 percent did so online.
- Twenty-one percent communicated with a government official about an important issue via phone, letter, or in person; 18 percent did so online via text or email.

- Seven percent expressed an opinion about a social or political issue on a live radio or TV show; 18 percent commented to a blog post or online news story about such an issue.
- Three percent sent a letter to the editor via regular mail, compared with 4 percent by text or e-mail.
- Thirty-nine percent of US adults participated in a political activity on a social networking site (SNS) such as Google+, Twitter, or Facebook; of these SNS-using adults:
    - 38 percent promoted material others have posted concerning social or political issues, compared with 23 percent of all adults;
    - 35 percent encouraged others to vote, compared with 21 percent of all adults;
    - 33 percent reposted content on social/political issues, compared with 19 percent of all adults;
    - 31 percent encouraged others to take action on important social/political issues, compared with 19 percent of all adults;
    - 28 percent posted links to political articles or stories, compared with 17 percent of all adults;
    - 21 percent belonged to a group working on social or political issues or advancing a cause, compared with 12 percent of all adults; and
    - 20 percent follow political candidates, elected officials, or other public figures, compared with 12 percent of all adults.
- In total, 66 percent of SNS-using adults indicated that they had participated in one or more of the above activities, compared with 39 percent of all adults.
- Two-thirds of all US eighteen- to twenty-four-year-olds and nearly three-fourths of those on SNS, had participated in social network–related political activity in the year before the survey.
- Political engagement on SNS sites increased significantly between 2008 and 2012:
    - Eleven percent of SNS users indicated that they had used such sites to post political news in 2008, increasing to 28 percent in 2012.

- Twelve percent of SNS users had followed or friended a political figure on SNS sites in 2008, increasing to 20 percent in 2012.
- Thirteen percent of users in 2008 had joined or started an SNS group organized around social or political issues in 2008, compared with 21 percent in 2012;
- Forty-three percent of SNS users were motivated by something they had read on a social networking site to learn more about a social or political issue.
- Eighteen percent of SNS users decided to take action on a social or political issue due to something they had read on a social networking site.
- Of politically oriented social networking site users,
  - 63 percent recently got involved in a political group or activity, compared with a national average of 48 percent;
  - 60 percent expressed opinions on social or political issues online, compared with a national average of 34 percent;
  - 53 percent expressed such an opinion offline (e.g., signing a petition or sending a letter to a government official), compared with a national average of 39 percent; and
  - 20 percent made a political contribution, compared with a national average of 16 percent.
- Altogether, 83 percent of political SNS users involved themselves in social or political issues outside of the social networking sites.
- Fifty-six percent of the US population has experienced one of the following effects of the economic downturn that began in 2008:
  - 46 percent have reduced the quality or amount of food they buy;
  - 38 percent have delayed dental or medical treatment; and
  - 25 percent have put off making a house payment or rent.

- Comparing the 56 percent of the US population who have been negatively affected by the economic downturn that started in 2008 to the 44 percent who have not been negatively affected:
  - Those affected are just as likely to use SNS or the Internet, to participate in political activity or groups in person, and to receive political calls to action;
  - 41 percent of those affected have spoken out about issues of importance to them, compared with 36 percent of those unaffected; and
  - 35 percent of those affected have encouraged others on SNS to take action on issues of importance to them, versus 27 percent of those unaffected.

The Pew Research Center for the People and the Press reported in July 2013 that

- 56 percent of those surveyed in the United States believed that federal courts were failing to adequately limit the Internet and telephone data collected by the government in the name of fighting terrorism;
- 70 percent believed the data collected was used for other purposes than fighting terrorism;
- 47 percent were most concerned that antiterrorism policies were excessively restricting the civil liberties of the average citizen, compared with 35 percent whose greatest concern was that antiterrorism policies were not going far enough to protect the nation;
- the percentage expressing greater concern over civil liberties has increased by fifteen percentage points since Pew first asked the question in October 2010;
- among those under the age of thirty, 60 percent rated their greatest concern as the restriction of civil liberties, compared with 29 percent whose greatest concern was that antiterrorism policies were not adequately protecting the nation; and
- 46 percent of young people approved of the government's extensive data collection programs while 49 percent disapproved.

According to a survey of 520 US writers conducted by public opinion research organization the FDR Group on behalf of PEN American Center (a literary and human rights organization), published in November 2013,

- 66 percent of writers disapproved of "the government's collection of telephone and Internet data as part of antiterrorism efforts" compared with 44 percent of the general public;
- 12 percent of writers approved of the data collection, compared with 50 percent of the general public;
- 85 percent of writers were concerned about US government surveillance of its citizens;
- 73 percent of writers were more concerned than they had ever been before about freedom of the press and the right to privacy;
- writers were engaging in self-censorship on sensitive subjects, such as mass incarceration, drug policies, the Occupy movement, and criticism of the government;
- 28 percent had avoided or reduced social media activities; an additional 12 percent had seriously considered it;
- 24 percent have avoided sensitive topics in e-mail conversations or phone calls, with another 9 percent seriously considering doing so; and
- 16 percent had avoided visiting websites or doing Internet searches on potentially suspicious or controversial subjects, with another 12 percent having seriously considered doing so.

Wealth Inequality and Income Insecurity in the United States

According to a November 2011 report in *Business Insider*, as of 2007,

- the bottom 50 percent of the US population had 2.5 percent of the nation's wealth;
- the 50th to 90th percentile had 26 percent of the wealth;
- the 91st to 99th percentile had 37.7 percent of the wealth; and
- the top 1 percent of the population had 33.8 percent of the wealth.

Chuck Collins, a senior scholar at the Institute for Policy Studies, reported in April 2012 that

- whereas in the mid-1970s, the top 1 percent received 8 percent of all income in the United States, by 2010 that had increased to 21 percent; and
- the four hundred wealthiest individuals in the United States now possessed more wealth than did the 150 million poorest people (nearly half the population) in the United States.

According to an article by Professor G. William Domhoff of the Sociology Department of the University of California at Santa Cruz, last updated in February 2013,

- 42 percent of all wealth created between 1983 and 2004 went to the top 1 percent of the population;
- 94 percent of all wealth created during that period went to the top 20 percent of the population; and
- only 6 percent of all wealth created during that period went to the bottom 80 percent of the population.

The US Department of Agriculture Food and Nutrition Service reported in 2013 that

- in fiscal year (FY) 2010, 40,301,878 people in the United States were using the Supplemental Nutrition Assistance Program (i.e., food stamps); and
- in FY 2013 that number had increased to 47,666,124 people.

A *U.S. News & World Report* article on October 16, 2012, reported that

- as of August 2012 only half of US households were middle-income, compared with 61 percent in the 1970s; and
- the richest 1 percent of US households now have 288 times as much wealth as the average middle-class US household.

The CNNMoney website reported on April 15, 2013, that

- CEOs in the largest US companies earned an average of $12.3 million in total pay in 2012, which is 354 times greater than the average US worker (who made $34,645 in 2012); and

- by comparison, in 1980 total CEO pay was 42 times greater than that of an average worker.

Pew Research Center for the People and the Press reported on September 12, 2013, that

- 63 percent of the US population believed the economic system was no more secure than it had been before the market crash in 2008;
- 72 percent said government policies after the recession started in 2008 had done little or nothing to help poor people;
- 71 percent said policies had done little or nothing to help the middle class;
- 67 percent said policies had done little to help small businesses;
- 69 percent said government policies had done a fair amount or a great deal to help financial institutions and large banks;
- 67 percent said policies had helped large corporations; and
- 59 percent said policies had helped rich people.

Social Conflict in Society

According to the Pew Research Center, reporting on surveys conducted in 2009, 2011, and 2012,

- in 2009, 47 percent of the US public felt that there were strong or very strong conflicts between the poor and the rich, increasing in 2011 to 66 percent and in 2012 to 58 percent;
- in 2009 and 2011, 55 percent said there were strong or very strong conflicts between immigrants and native-born people, whereas in 2012, 62 percent felt that way;
- in 2009 and 2011, 39 percent of those polled felt there was strong or very strong conflict between blacks and whites; in 2012, 38 percent felt that way;
- in 2009, 25 percent of respondents felt there was strong or very strong conflict between young and old people, whereas

in 2011, 34 percent felt that way, and in 2012, 29 percent felt that away; and

- in 2011, 81 percent believed there was strong or very strong conflict between Democrats and Republicans.

The Gallup polling organization reported in 2013 that

- in October 2013 only 18 percent of Americans surveyed described themselves as satisfied with the way things were going in the United States;
- the average satisfaction rating since Gallup first started asking the question in 1979 was 38 percent;
- in 1998 and 2000, during an economic boom, the satisfaction rating hit 60 percent;
- the lowest average was 15 percent during the economic crisis of 2008; and
- the second-lowest average was 17 percent in 2011, during the Occupy protests.

According to a 2013 article by Professor Erica Chenoweth, associate senior researcher at the Peace Research Institute of Oslo, Norway, based on a study she did of three hundred violent and nonviolent resistance campaigns around the world from 1900 to 2006,

- violent political resistance movements had had a success rate of 26 percent;
- nonviolent movements had had a success rate of 53 percent; and
- all of the campaigns that had had a participation rate of at least 3.5 percent (in the United States that would amount to 11 million people) of the population were successful.

What You Should Do About Social Protest

Gather Information

The first step in grappling with any complex and controversial issue is to be informed about it. Gather as much information as you can, from a variety of sources, on whatever social protest movement(s) you are interested in. The essays in this book form an excellent starting point, representing a variety of viewpoints and approaches to the topic. Your school or local library will be another source of useful information; look there for relevant books, magazines, and encyclopedia entries. The bibliography and Organizations to Contact section of this book will give you useful starting points in gathering additional information.

There is a wealth of information available on every conceivable social protest movement. Popular areas of social protest include climate change, wealth inequality, gay rights, government surveillance, drug prohibition, and many more. Internet search engines will be helpful to you in your search. There are many blogs and websites that cover the causes championed by protest movements from a variety of perspectives, including concerned individuals offering their opinions and advice, advocacy and activist organizations, popular media outlets, and governmental and scientific organizations. The proliferation of digital technology has enabled a massive increase in the information and perspectives being shared on every conceivable topic.

Identify the Issues Involved

Once you have gathered your information, review it methodically to discover the key issues involved. If climate change, for example, is an area of concern for you, consider questions such as: What evidence is there that the climate has already begun to change? What do qualified experts have to say about it? How might climate change in your lifetime or further into the future, and what will be the likely consequences for you or future generations? Is this a problem that needs to be addressed, and if so, what can be done to improve the situation? If some—perhaps severe—degree of climate change is now inevitable, how can humans adapt to it? What is being done about the issue by various levels of government, corporations, protest organizations, etc.? How can a concerned individual get involved? Consider all sides of any issue(s) you are taking an interest in.

Evaluate Your Information Sources

In developing your own opinion, it is vital to evaluate the sources of the information you have discovered. Authors of books, magazine articles, and so forth, however well intentioned, have their own perspectives and biases that may affect how they present information on the subject. In some cases people and organizations may deliberately or inadvertently distort information to support a strongly held ideological or moral position—signs of this include oversimplification and extreme positions.

For example, if you are focusing on income inequality, you may find arguments from those advocating low taxes for corporations and the wealthy that income inequality is not a problem in the United States because income mobility is very high—that is, a high percentage of people move from one income bracket to another (either up or down) during their lifetimes, so that someone who is in the poorest 20 percent of the population may later become a member of the wealthiest 1 percent. They may ignore or downplay evidence that in the vast majority of cases, people who move from one income category to another move by an insignificant amount and that going from very poor to rich is quite rare. Or perhaps you are interested in issues of privacy and surveillance. A representative of an intelligence-gathering agency such as the National Security Agency (NSA) may justify widespread surveillance based on the need to protect the nation from foreign attack but may minimize or ignore the importance of threats to privacy; conversely, a privacy advocate may minimize the importance of intelligence agencies' ability to gather information for national security reasons.

If you find someone arguing against their expected bias—for example, an environmental activist advocating nuclear power to combat climate change, or a police chief advocating an end to drug prohibition—it may be worthwhile to pay particular attention to what they are saying as they are likely to have reached their position without bias. Always critically evaluate and assess your sources rather than take whatever they say at face value.

Examine Your Own Perspective

Consider your own beliefs, feelings, and biases on whatever social protest issues you are investigating. Perhaps you have been influenced by the attitudes of family or friends or media reports. Beware of the tendency to look for perspectives and information that confirm what you already believe to be true and to discount anything that contradicts your viewpoint. Counter this tendency by seeking out and seriously considering attitudes that differ from your own. Find people who disagree with you on an issue you consider important but are willing to engage in respectful dialogue or debate on the issue. Listen deeply and openly to what they have to say, and really consider their position. Even if you continue to disagree with them, you will have a deeper understanding of the issue, as well as your own biases and blind spots. The insight you gain may also help you find more effective ways of communicating your message to those with different worldviews and new approaches to your cause that may benefit everyone.

Form Your Own Opinion and Take Action

Once you have gathered and organized the information, identified the issues involved, and examined your own perspective, you will be ready to form an opinion and to advocate that position in debates and discussions, and—if you wish—to take concrete action to advance particular causes that you believe in. Regardless of the conclusions you come to on important issues, you can find people and organizations with similar attitudes who are striving to make changes in the world in accordance with those beliefs—check out the Organizations to Contact section of this book for some starting points. If you would like to contact your political representatives directly to tell them what you think about important social or political issues of the day, the website www.usa.gov /Contact/Elected.shtml can help you get started.

ORGANIZATIONS TO CONTACT

The editors have compiled the following list of organizations concerned with the issues debated in this book. The descriptions are derived from materials provided by the organizations. All have publications or information available for interested readers. The list was compiled on the date of publication of the present volume; names, addresses, phone and fax numbers, and e-mail and Internet addresses may change. Be aware that many organizations take several weeks or longer to respond to inquiries, so allow as much time as possible.

American Civil Liberties Union (ACLU)
125 Broad St., 18th Fl.
New York, NY 1004
(212) 549-2500
e-mail: aclu@aclu.org
website: www.aclu.org

The ACLU works daily in courts, legislatures, and communities to defend and preserve the individual rights and liberties that the US Constitution and laws of the United States guarantee everyone. The organization's website features information on key issues such as "Fair Justice, Smart Justice," which works to improve America's criminal justice system; "Protecting Civil Liberties in the Digital Age"; "Defending Targets of Discrimination"; and "Keep America Safe and Free," which addresses civil liberty issues associated with the war on terror, including torture, censorship, and discrimination. Specific problems addressed by the ACLU include prison conditions, surveillance and privacy, and marijuana law reform. Of particular interest is the section on the right to protest. The ACLU website also offers the *ACLU Action Newsletter*, e-mail alerts, and video, podcasts, and infographics.

Compassion Over Killing (COK)
PO Box 9773
Washington, DC 20016
(301) 891-2458
e-mail: info@cok.net
website: www.cok.net

COK is a national nonprofit animal advocacy organization head-
quartered in Washington, DC, with an additional office in Los
Angeles. Working to end animal abuse since 1995, COK focuses
on cruelty to animals in agriculture and promotes a vegetarian diet
as a way to build a kinder world for both humans and animals. Its
website features reports on undercover investigations into animal
cruelty in agribusiness, a blog, the magazine *Compassionate Action*,
an electronic newsletter, a free "Vegetarian Starter Guide," and
links to vegetarian and animal rights news.

Drug Free America Foundation
5999 Central Ave., Ste. 301
Saint Petersburg, FL 33710
(727) 828-0211
fax: (727) 828-0212
e-mail: webmaster@dfaf.org
website: www.dfaf.org

Drug Free America Foundation is a nongovernmental drug pre-
vention and policy organization committed to developing, promoting, and sustaining global strategies, policies, and laws that
will reduce illegal drug use, drug addiction, and drug-related
injuries and deaths. Its reference collection contains more than
twenty-one hundred books and other media chronicling the rise
of the drug culture and current drug policy issues. It favors the
war on drugs, and its website contains many articles defending
current policy, including student drug testing.

Drug Policy Alliance
131 W. Thirty-Third St., 15th Fl.
New York, NY 10001

(212) 613-8020
fax: (212) 613-8021
e-mail: nyc@drugpolicy.org
website: www.drugpolicy.org

The Drug Policy Alliance believes in the sovereignty of individuals over their own minds and bodies. Its position is that people should be punished for crimes committed against others but not for using marijuana or other drugs as a personal choice. The alliance, an independent nonprofit organization, supports and publicizes alternatives to current US policies on illegal drugs, including marijuana. To keep Americans informed, the Drug Policy Alliance compiles newspaper articles on drug legalization issues and distributes legislative updates. Its website features a blog and the *Ally* newsletter. Of particular note is the website's section on medical marijuana, which includes a "Resources" section and an "Activist Toolkit."

Girls for Gender Equity (GGE)
30 Third Ave., Ste. 103
Brooklyn, NY 11217
(718) 857-1393
fax: (718) 857-2239
e-mail: info@ggenyc.org
website: www.ggenyc.org

GGE is a nonprofit organization committed to the physical, psychological, social, and economic development of girls and women. Through education, organizing, and physical fitness, GGE encourages communities to remove barriers and create opportunities for girls and women to live self-determined lives. Its website offers the newsletter *GGE Friends* and has a section on sexual harassment. GGE published *Hey, Shorty! A Guide to Combating Sexual Harassment and Violence in Schools and on the Streets*.

Global Exchange
2017 Mission St., 2nd Fl.
San Francisco, CA 94110
(415) 255-7296

fax: (415) 255-7498
e-mail: web@globalexchange.org
website: www.globalexchange.org

Global Exchange is a human rights organization that exposes economic and political injustice around the world. It supports education, activism, and a noninterventionist US foreign policy. Its "Stop Funding War" campaign seeks to inspire creative actions to expose the real cost of war at home and abroad, challenge war profiteering and military recruitment, and build people-to-people ties to expand understanding and tolerance. The organization's website offers a blog network, e-mail updates, and a section on ways to get involved.

Greenpeace
702 H St. NW, Ste. 300
Washington, DC 20001
(800) 722-6995
e-mail: info@wdc.greenpeace.org
website: www.greenpeace.org

Greenpeace was formed in 1971 when a small group of activists chartered a fishing boat and set off to protest nuclear testing off the coast of Alaska. Its mission is to use peaceful protest and creative communication to expose global environmental problems and to promote solutions that are essential to a green and peaceful future. The organization continues to stage peaceful protests against the use of nuclear power while standing up for renewable energy sources. Other areas of its focus include protecting ancient forests and the ocean. Greenpeace seeks to educate policy makers and the international public by publishing annual reports and fact sheets on environmental topics such as climate change and nuclear energy. The organization's website includes volunteer opportunities, a blog called *The Witness*, and a multimedia section.

Habitat for Humanity International
121 Habitat St.
Americus, GA 31709-3498
(800) 422-4828

e-mail: youthprograms@habitat.org
website: www.habitat.org

Habitat for Humanity is a nonprofit ecumenical Christian ministry that believes that every man, woman, and child should have a decent, safe, and affordable place to live. The organization helps to construct houses for some of the nearly 100 million homeless people around the world, as well as the nearly 2 billion people who live in slum housing. Its website offers a variety of information on its projects. Of special interest is the section "Habitat Youth Programs," which offers a variety of ways that youth can get involved.

HollaBack
30 Third Ave., #800B
Brooklyn, NY 11217
(347) 889-5510
e-mail: holla@ihollaback.org
website: www.ihollaback.org

Hollaback is a nonprofit organization leading a global movement to end sexual harassment on the streets. A network of local activists around the world collaborate to better understand street harassment, ignite public conversations, and develop innovative strategies to ensure equal access to public spaces. Hollaback has empowered people in over fifty cities and twenty countries to respond through a smartphone/web application. Users are encouraged to speak up when they see harassment by quickly documenting it in a short (photo optional) post and sharing it to a publicly viewable map. The Hollaback website features stories of harassment and efforts to counteract harassment from around the world. The website's resources page includes book recommendations, articles, videos, how-to guides, research, and Android and iPhone apps for download.

Man Up Campaign
79 Fifth Ave., 4th Fl.
New York, NY 10003
(646) 862-2854
website: http://manupcampaign.org

The Man Up Campaign aims to engage youth in a global movement to end gender-based violence and advance gender equality through youth-led initiatives intended to transform communities, nations, and the world by promoting gender equality and sensitivity among global youth and building a community of like-minded individuals, initiatives, and organizations. Issues addressed include sexual harassment, psychological and emotional abuse, and rape. Man Up Campaign maintains a presence on Twitter, Facebook, and YouTube. Visitors to its website register to be notified of events, information, and opportunities in their country.

Men Can Stop Rape (MCSR)
1003 K St. NW, Ste. 200
Washington, DC 20001
(202) 265-6530
fax: (202) 265-4362
e-mail: info@mencanstoprape.org
website: www.mencanstoprape.org

MCSR is a nonprofit organization based in Washington, DC, whose mission is to mobilize men to use their strength for creating cultures free from violence, especially men's violence against women. Rather than helping women reduce their risk of being victims of men's violence, the organization focuses on helping boys and men use their strength in positive ways in all of their relationships. MCSR founded the Men of Strength (MOST) Club, a school-based twenty-two-week curriculum teaching males aged eleven to eighteen healthy dating relationship skills and encouraging them to show their "strength" in positive ways among their peers. It also distributes posters and other information designed to empower middle school–aged boys to take action against gender-based harassment, teasing, bullying, and cyberbullying. The MCSR website offers a newsletter, news items, videos, and handouts.

Mobilize.org
1029 Vermont Ave. NW, Ste. 600
Washington, DC 20005
(202) 400-3848

e-mail: info@mobilize.org
website: http://mobilize.org

Mobilize.org is an organization created to empower and invest in millenials (young adults born between the years 1976 and 1996) to create and implement solutions to social problems. It accomplishes this by training millennial activists, investing in groups working on solutions to world problems, and facilitating meetings of millennials to discuss important social issues. The organization's website features a blog with news of interest to all young activists, including the blog entry "Never Too Young: Activist Leadership in Millennial Teens."

National Student Campaign Against Hunger and Homelessness
328 S. Jefferson St., Ste. 620
Chicago, IL 60661
(312) 544-4436, ext. 204
fax: (312) 275-7150
e-mail: info@studentsagainsthunger.org
website: www.studentsagainsthunger.org

Founded in 1985 by state Public Interest Research Groups (PIRGs), the campaign is committed to ending hunger and homelessness in America by educating, engaging, and training high school and college students to directly meet individuals' immediate needs while advocating for long-term systemic solutions. The organization offers training materials and fact sheets, information about hunger and homelessness, and opportunities for volunteers.

Sustainable Table
c/o GRACE Communications Foundation
215 Lexington Ave.
New York, NY 10016
(212) 726-9161
e-mail: info@sustainabletable.org
website: www.sustainabletable.org

Sustainable Table was established in 2003 to promote sustainable food and educate consumers about food-related issues. The organization produced a popular video called the Meatrix, which (along with two sequels) humorously educates consumers about the problems caused by factory farms. Sustainable Table also offers an Eat Well Guide that lists more than twenty-five thousand sustainable food resources in the United States and Canada, as well as the blog *Ecocentric*, which covers food, water, and energy issues. The group's website also includes a podcast and links to web videos on sustainability.

350.org
20 Jay St., Ste. 1010
Brooklyn, NY 11201
(518) 635-0350
e-mail: team@350.org
website: www.350.org

An international campaign, 350.org works to build a movement to unite the world around solutions to the climate crisis. It aims to get the global atmosphere below 350 parts per million (ppm) of carbon dioxide (CO_2), which it says is the highest safe level in terms of the greenhouse effect (as of October 2013, the level of CO_2 in the atmosphere was over 393 ppm). Evidence supporting this claim is provided as well as many ideas on what can be done to achieve this goal.

United for Peace and Justice (UFPJ)
PO Box 607, Times Square Station
New York, NY 10108
(212) 868-5545
e-mail: info.ufpj@gmail.com
website: www.unitedforpeace.org

UFPJ opposes preemptive wars of aggression and rejects any drive to expand US control over other nations and to strip Americans of rights at home under the cover of fighting terrorism and spreading democracy. It rejects the use of war and racism to concentrate power in the hands of the few. The UFPJ website publishes news articles, essays, and information on recent antiwar events and has working groups focusing on specific issues such as Afghanistan and nuclear abolition. People can also sign up to receive UFPJ Action Alerts, which provide updates and ways to get involved in the work of the organization, member groups, and allies.

Waging Nonviolence (WNV)
500 Washington Ave., #52
Brooklyn, NY 11238
e-mail: contact@wagingnonviolence.org
website: http://wagingnonviolence.org

WNV is a source for original news and analysis about struggles for justice and peace around the globe, highlighting the use of nonviolent strategies and tactics in achieving social and political change. The organization's website includes a blog, a weekly e-mail newsletter, information on conflict resolution, experiments in nonviolent protest, and diverse articles on nonviolent social protest movements around the world. Most material on the WNV website, unless otherwise noted, is published under a Creative Commons Attribution–Share Alike 3.0 license, which permits free reuse and adaptation as long as WNV and the author are noted as the source of the material.

War Child North America
489 College St. West, Ste. 500
Toronto, ON M6G 1A5
Canada
(416) 971-7474
fax: (416) 971-7946; toll free: (866) WARCHILD
e-mail: info@warchild.ca
website: www.warchild.ca

War Child's mission is to empower children and young people to flourish within their communities and overcome the challenges of living with, and recovering from, conflict. Its goals include increasing access to education, especially for girls and young women; creating a protective environment for the rights of children and youth; and ultimately working toward a world where no child knows war. Its website offers a newsletter, information on its programs in Afghanistan and other countries, and a section on how high school students can get involved.

Win Without War
2000 M St. NW, Ste. 720
Washington, DC 20036
(202) 232-3317
e-mail: info@winwithoutwar.org
website: www.winwithoutwar.org

Win Without War is a forty-member coalition of organizations formed in 2002 to lead the first national campaign against the war in Iraq. Its current aims include working to demilitarize Afghanistan and close the Guantánamo Bay detention facility. The organization's website features a blog, a Twitter feed, multimedia presentations, e-mail updates, and information sections on conflict in Afghanistan, Iraq, Iran, and Pakistan.

Youth for Human Rights International (YHRI)
1920 Hillhurst Ave., #416
Los Angeles, CA 90027
(323) 663-5799
website: www.youthforhumanrights.org

YHRI is a nonprofit organization founded in 2001 by Mary Shuttleworth, an educator born and raised in apartheid South Africa, where she witnessed firsthand the devastating effects of discrimination and the lack of basic human rights. The purpose of YHRI is to teach youth about human rights, specifically the United Nations' Universal Declaration of Human Rights, and inspire them to become advocates for tolerance and peace. YHRI includes hundreds of groups, clubs, and chapters around the world. The YHRI website offers information on how young people can take action in their communities to advocate for human rights; a section "Voices for Human Rights," which describes contributions made by human rights champions such as First Lady Eleanor

Roosevelt and civil rights activist Martin Luther King Jr.; YHRI news; and one-minute videos depicting the thirty Articles of the Universal Declaration of Human Rights. YHRI also makes available a free information kit for educators to teach youth about human rights.

BIBLIOGRAPHY

Books

Steve Brodner, *Artists Against the War*. Nevada City, CA: Underwood, 2010.

Steve Crawshaw and John Jackson, *Small Acts of Resistance: How Courage, Tenacity, and Ingenuity Can Change the World*. New York: Union Square, 2010.

Benjamin Dickson, Hunt Emerson, and Sean Michael Wilson, *Fight the Power! A Visual History of Protest Amongst the English-Speaking Peoples*. Oxford: New Internationalist, 2013.

Jane Drake and Ann Love, *Yes You Can! Your Guide to Becoming an Activist*. Toronto, ON: Tundra, 2010.

Sarah van Gelder, ed., *This Changes Everything: Occupy Wall Street and the 99% Movement*. San Francisco: Berrett-Koehler, 2011.

Todd Gitlin, *Occupy Nation: The Roots, the Spirit, and the Promise of Occupy Wall Street*. New York: itbooks, 2012.

Mikki Halpin, *It's Your World—If You Don't Like It, Change It: Activism for Teenagers*. New York: Simon Pulse, 2004.

Mark Hawthorne, *Striking at the Roots: A Practical Guide to Animal Activism*. Winchester, UK: Changemakers, 2007.

Dallas Jessup and Rusty Fischer, *Young Revolutionaries Who Rock: An Insider's Guide to Saving the World One Revolution at a Time*. Portland, OR: Sutton Hart, 2009.

Cathryn Berger Kaye and Philippe Cousteau, *Going Blue: A Teen Guide to Saving Our Oceans, Lakes, Rivers & Wetlands*. Minneapolis: Free Spirit, 2010.

Ken Kolsbun and Michael S. Sweeney, *Peace: The Biography of a Symbol*. Washington, DC: National Geographic, 2008.

Barbara A. Lewis, *The Teen Guide to Global Action: How to Connect with Others (Near & Far) to Create Social Change*. Minneapolis: Free Spirit, 2007.

Dorian Lynskey, *33 Revolutions per Minute: A History of Protest Songs, from Billie Holiday to Green Day*. New York: Ecco, 2011.

Vanessa Martir, Nancy Lublin, and Julia Steers, *Do Something! A Handbook for Young Activists*. New York: Workman, 2010.

Bill McKibben, *Fight Global Warming Now: The Handbook for Taking Action in Your Community*. New York: Holt, 2007.

Barry Miles, *Peace: 50 Years of Protest*. Pleasantville, NY: Reader's Digest, 2008.

Elizabeth Partridge, *Marching for Freedom: Walk Together, Children, and Don't You Grow Weary*. New York: Viking, 2009.

Sharon J. Smith, *The Young Activist's Guide to Building a Green Movement + Changing the World*. Berkeley, CA: Ten Speed, 2011.

Astra Taylor, *Occupy! Scenes from Occupied America*. London: Verso, 2011.

Periodicals & Internet Sources

Bim Adewunmi, "Sexualized Femen Protest 'Naive and Foolish at Best,'" CNN Opinion, April 22, 2013. www.cnn.com.

Peter Beaumont, "How Mass Protests Around the Globe Have Become the 'New Social Network,'" *New Zealand Herald*, June 24, 2013.

Medea Benjamin, "A Heckler's Guide: How Those in Power Should Handle Protest," *The Guardian* (Manchester, UK), June 6, 2013.

David Brin, "Sousveillance: A New Era for Police Accountability," *Open Salon* (blog), *Salon*, June 18, 2011. http://open.salon.com.

Tom Chatfield, "Manifesto for a Virtual Revolution: Cyber-Activist Cory Doctorow's New Novel Imagines a Revolt of Online Slaves," *The Independent* (London), May 21, 2010.

Erica Chenoweth, "The Dissident's Toolkit," *Foreign Policy*, October 25, 2013.

Steve Crawshaw and John Jackson, "10 Everyday Acts of Resistance That Changed the World," *Yes!*, April 1, 2011.

The Economist, "The Digital Demo: Technology Makes Protests More Likely, but Not Yet More Effective," June 29, 2013.

Richard Eskow, "Where the Hell Is the Outrage?," Campaign for America's Future, July 9, 2013. http://ourfuture.org.

Sarah van Gelder, "Climate Change Is Happening but We Can Meet the Challenge," *The Guardian* (Manchester, UK), June 8, 2013.

Malcolm Gladwell, "Small Change: Why the Revolution Will Not Be Tweeted," *New Yorker*, October 4, 2010.

Tom H. Hastings, "Branding Your Movement: Think Outside the Mask," *Hastings on Nonviolence* (blog), June 23, 2013. http://hastingsnonviolence.blogspot.com.

Mathew Ingram, "Gladwell Still Missing the Point About Social Media and Activism," Gigaom, February 3, 2011. http://gigaom.com.

Philip Kennicott, "UC Davis Pepper-Spraying Raises Questions About Role of Police," *Washington Post*, November 20, 2011.

Naomi Klein, "How Science Is Telling Us All to Revolt," *New Statesman*, October 29, 2013.

John Knefel, "Meet the Private Companies Helping Cops Spy on Protesters," *Rolling Stone*, October 24, 2013.

Ronald J. Krotoszynski, "Protecting Face-to-Face Protest," *New York Times*, April 9, 2012, p. A21.

Susan Lin, "Never Too Young: Activist Leadership in Millennial Teens," Mobilize.org, February 7, 2013. http://mobilize.org.

New Internationalist, "Is It OK for Protesters to Damage Property?," March 1, 2011.

Vanessa Ortiz, "Where Are the Women?," *Sojourners*, April 29, 2011.

Jon Queally, "In Chicago, Students Rise Up Against Corporate Assault on Public Education," Common Dreams, July 25, 2013. www.commondreams.org.

Ted Rall, "Why Are Americans So Passive? Get Pissed Off and Break Things," *Common Dreams*, June 22, 2013. www.com mondreams.org.

Molly Sauter, "The Future of Civil Disobedience Online," *io9*, June 17, 2013. http://io9.com.

Andrew Ross Sorkin, "Occupy Wall Street: A Frenzy That Fizzled," *New York Times*, September 17, 2012.

Kelley Vlahos, "Occupying a Footnote to History: What Really Brought Down the OWS Movement?," *American Conservative*, September 19, 2012.

Tom Watson, "Occupy Wall Street's Year: Three Outcomes for the History Books," *Forbes*, September 17, 2012.

Mark Weisbrot, "Domestic Dissent Can Change US Foreign Policy for the Better," *The Guardian* (Manchester, UK), June 17, 2013.

Juan Williams, "The Trayvon Martin Tragedies," *Wall Street Journal*, March 27, 2012.

Stephen Zunes, "Weapons of Mass Democracy: Nonviolent Resistance Is the Most Powerful Tactic Against Oppressive Regimes," *Yes!*, September 16, 2009.

INDEX